Very Personal Stories

Jeffrey Ellinger

ISBN: 069290526X
ISBN 13: 9780692905265

"Dying for love might be pitiable, but it wasn't much different, finally, from any other kind of dying." — Richard Yates, Cold Spring Harbor

To anyone in yearning

Worry

My worry is that I have received the right amount of attention. I have not been underrated. The menial jobs I have worked are the jobs I was qualified to work and not the jobs I had to take because I needed to support my dreams. I worry I am getting what I deserve, that I am balding because bad things happen to bad people, and balding is as bad as it can get. I worry nothing I have written has been underappreciated by anyone. I worry this world is going to end in nuclear war. I worry that that's just as well. If we lived in peace we'd just make too many of us and end in starvation. I worry I am receiving the portion I should receive, and that it wasn't some kind of bad luck every time I wanted someone who didn't want me. I worry the exact order of events that were supposed to happen happened, and no matter if I'd done things according to every guidebook in the world, the one opposite me would have left for another.

Patience

With patience I'd have never released a book with typos and rhyming words. I'd have paid a real editor to edit my novel about online dating, not a one-time friend-with-benefits who smokes too much weed and made me weak with her eye-watering, somehow always tan backside. With patience the beautiful Asian in Brooklyn would have loved my self-published novel and not been "pulled out of the story occasionally." With patience, my prose would not have been so doggerel. More patience, and money. That's how people succeed, along with cutthroat skulduggery. If I'd just studied for the GRE ten years ago and gotten into a marginal MFA school I could be a notable author, my books with a small press by now, while I scramble to survive on opinion pieces appearing on websites. With no patience as a young man, I flitted from job to job and eventually landed on self-published novelist, and that isn't even a job. I started a blog and it got me nowhere, like using a stair climber in a gym thinking I was climbing a mountain. What a character flaw, to not have patience. With patience as an online dater I would have found The One, so fit, who smelled like fresh laundry and sandalwood and wore high-waisted skirts in 2010 and had a job after college at an advertising firm in Minneapolis. She wrote novels too, but deferred to me, since she knew the most important thing, what she loved about me most. You already know.

Marshmallows

From a famous study about marshmallows you learn that if, when you were little, you didn't take a marshmallow offered to you in the little room with nothing else to eat—if you could wait—your life is now perfect. But if you ate the marshmallow right away, you are now a craven sybarite who will never have true lasting joy. The only happiness that will come for you in adulthood is when you are old enough to find a job as a data entry specialist, and you have enough money left over from self-publishing your novels, and you can afford to buy all the marshmallows you please. You can stand there in your pantry and enjoy, and when one handful is gone you reach in and have another. No one is stopping you.

Emotional Joseph

While walking to the bar that night Joseph hoped things would be different, but as they ate their hamburgers and drank their beers, he had to admit—much later, when being honest with himself—the night mirrored their years of working together: at first businesslike, for a short time happy, then, as in their final dying days, full of disappointment and pain. Their food was mostly eaten, runt fries shoved to the borders of their plates. Torn pieces of beer labels strewn like unraked leaves on the gouged table. Behind them in a booth, a rowdy group of middle-aged folks sang "Hello" by Adele, off-key but in unison.

"Let me get this straight," Don said. Don had been the manager of the bookstore where they once worked. He hired Joseph. Rebecca, too. "You're asking if a woman orgasms in the process of conceiving her child...you're asking if her child is more or less likely to live a happy life? Am I getting this right?"

"Yesss," Joseph slurred. "She comes, this is good, or this is bad...for the child."

"Oh my gosh," Rebecca said, and slapped her forehead for emphasis. She had curly hair, red lips, and freckles below her collarbone. She took her husband's hand and began to knead his knuckles steadily.

"Okay," Don said, accepting his wife's encouragement. "It's a good thing. To, well, to do that. But it's not possible to improve the life of an unborn baby. Not scientifically plausible."

"That's a goddamn boring view," Joseph said, slamming his beer. Playfully, he would say. "Don't you two believe in the power of an orgasm?" He'd been drinking, the couple knew, before coming to the bar. "Whatever it is, the juices of life or whatever, that has to flow through to the baby, right? It's like being born under a good sign. So, let me ask you two…"

Rebecca tilted her head, and now Joseph could grin coyly and act like he was joking, but he couldn't pretend. He was the one who'd shouted, years ago, "I think Rebecca is great!" at the end of the second week of closing the store with her. And he had cried the night Rebecca explained in the parking lot how it was "just going to have to be." And he was definitely the one who'd knocked over an endcap of puzzles the day he quit, leaving everyone in the store, including the two workers behind the counter, Don and Rebecca, speechless.

Rebecca loosened her posture. "A gentleman never reveals these things," she said, taking Don's chin, and gave him a kiss on the lips, then small ones, over and over, on his cheek.

Now all that could be left was saliva, but still Joseph tipped back his beer. Then he tipped it back again, drinking the last warm bubbles of alcohol and spit. He placed it on the table and began to fiddle with what remained of the label. Rebecca tried a false smile. Turning to her husband, she saw Don summoning an invisible waiter. They sat in silence. Neither Rebecca nor Don had drunk so much that the night needed to be prolonged. Joseph was walking home. So they split the check. They paid, and when they got up to leave Joseph had his chance. At last he could give Rebecca a tender look, intimate. So he did, but she didn't reciprocate. Her cordiality shot through Joseph and everything that had ever happened made him wish he could rip out his guts and have them picked apart so someone in the world other than himself could know how much he felt. They walked out.

Outside, Rebecca chattered her teeth while Don stood like a statue. Joseph seemed to be the warmest of the bunch. He spoke first.

"We should do this thing more often, now that I'm back in town."

"We'd love that, Joseph," Rebecca said, and Don nodded. Time for a goodbye. Joseph, a man the couple would take pains to avoid for the rest of their life, gave one short wave, but they had already turned.

Obsessive Jerry

When he realized the receipt had fallen out of his pocket, Jerry Finke thought, *I could die right now.*

That's Jerry pushing a grocery cart with his girlfriend, Rachel Cohen, beside him. She walks obliviously, talking as Jerry scans the area to try and figure out where the receipt has gone. What a shock for her, to see her man rummaging for a scrap of paper among other scraps of paper and plastic bags on the embankment of gravely snow near his car, but that's all Jerry wanted to do. If he'd gone shopping by himself, he would have. Finding the receipt would be worth it, if it meant a clean slate in his mind. If he tried now and she asked, he wouldn't have an answer, and Jerry didn't want to mess this up. He understood how much of a blessing she was. If she saw him running after a small piece of paper, among trash in a ditch near a grocery store, she'd think he was crazy, which he was but could not say. Still, he wanted to find it and pick it up, maybe more than anything. It had fallen out of his pocket and he was sure it'd be his fault if someone got into an accident because the receipt flew into their windshield. They'd veer into another car, or, *Jesus,* Jerry thought as he put the groceries in the trunk of Rachel's car, *a boy or girl.* He'd seen kids riding their bikes in the area. Of course Jerry wouldn't be able to know for sure that this terrible accident had been his fault, but it was coming, he knew that. *Maybe*, he thought, as Rachel drove them home, *I could make a sign and stick it in the ditch on the side of the road.*

> My name is Jerry. I live at 8975 Oakdale Terrace. My phone number is 612-555-6565. If you've been in an accident on this street because of a small piece of paper flying into your windshield or know of someone who has, please, call me. It's my fault.

Jerry was soothed for a second in the silence of the car, thinking of the sign. He wondered if maybe he should itemize the receipt: a six-pack of beer, a bottle of vodka, and two organic ciders. Then he thought, *no*, he would take the fall no matter what. He was as culpable as the next guy. Somebody should own up. May as well be Jerry, the man with an artist girlfriend he didn't deserve, who almost managed a hotel, who enjoyed the '90s rock bands Pearl Jam and Sunny Day Real Estate. That Jerry, it may as well be him. The thought implanted in his brain, and when they got home, instead of putting away the groceries in bliss, Jerry retreated to formulate a plan.

Find a heavy black Sharpie and one of those canvases Rachel had lying around, how would he explain? Looking to doodle? Jerry was not an artist, and that's what Rachel liked about him, that he was a man who made money and had a nice head of hair and was good in bed, most of the time. He would need to go and buy one of those lawn signs they use to promote politicians. To ensure that if anything ever did go wrong on that street by the grocery store, Jerry would get a call.

"Honey," Rachel said in the kitchen. She had received a grant for her art and now worked at home during the week. "You should start frying up your meat or it won't be ready in time. You know how I like your meat warm." And she tugged at his belt.

Jerry could only respond with a cheesy grin and wish that he could kiss her like she deserved to be, without reservation. But it was like someone pulled back on his lips. Not long ago, as he drove down a busy road, all the thoughts had come like needles: *You're too close to that bike, you made him fall. Now the rocks you're driving over are spraying all over those people and you don't know it but they're going to go blind and you're just going to go to work like nothing happened.*

Every day Jerry would go home to his basement apartment and drink to drown the thoughts. There were years like that, then one day in that blank time he happened to see an old lady putting groceries into her trunk, and he thought, *If I keep driving now, I could slice her in half. I could end things for us.*

That was some time ago and Jerry had improved. He got a job at a hotel. He sold his car and started running to work. He became more confident and moved up from the front-desk clerk to a manager, answering only to the man who answered to the man who owned the hotel. Those accomplishments earned Jerry enough money to go on a trip to Bahamas, just months ago. He thought, as Rachel cooked beside him: *I won't make it. This time I won't survive.*

"How's your meat coming?" Rachel asked as she kneaded the dough. The others, Jerry thought, had been so stupid to let this dough not be theirs to share with Rachel. Just then, Jerry noticed one of Rachel's freckles, and for a moment the sign and the receipt disappeared and he felt a deep love for her and the world. In the next, all the bad things came back and he began to cultivate the right excuse to leave.

How much time would he need to find a place that sold those placards, then to write the message and put it in the ground? And once he had taken those steps in the right order, in just the right way, all the thoughts would stop spinning, he convinced himself, and his stomach would stop boiling when he thought of the receipt floating in the wind—dancing across the snow, popping out from behind a parked car and smacking into a windshield—and at last he could just think of her, Rachel, with brown eyes and olive skin and a shapely backside.

"You know," Jerry said, as he began to finger through his wallet. "I might've gotten shorted at the grocery store." He thumbed ones and fives as if there were supposed to be a twenty. "I don't have my twenty."

"Really?" she asked.

"Yeah," Jerry said. "I don't have it. I should go back. Maybe I dropped it?"

"Oh Jerry, you'll never find it. Just stay."

"But I should try and see if I can get it, no? It'll be real quick, then we'll eat the most amazing pizza in the world." And he gave Rachel a kiss in her hair, and a hug from behind as he breathed her in deep.

Ten minutes later, Jerry drove away, remembering the old lady he'd seen putting her groceries in the trunk. It had been one of the last weeks at his old job and one of the last times he had driven his now-sold Malibu. As the car drifted, the voices quieted, then he pulled back to the road and they got louder again. He straightened out just in time.

He bought a wooden stake stapled to a heavy white canvas, and a thick black marker. "Steady now," he said as he left Staples. He gritted his teeth in the car. Soon he could go back and eat pizza and be happy, quelled.

After parking near the grocery store, he thought about how they met, when Rachel had just gotten out of the pool. She strolled in the sunshine to the bar and ordered a drink, her hair wrapped in a white towel. She had a belly-button ring, and he got the nerve to talk to her. Even more amazingly they ended up in a luxurious bed together the next morning. Everything changed as they ate room-service breakfast and she said, "I live in Minneapolis too."

The sign was done. Jerry sat in his car. Everyone in the neighborhood would have his phone number and his address and, more than that, *what if an authority figure sees this?* Jerry didn't want to go to a hospital. His grandma, who died long before Jerry was born, received electroshock therapy in the '50s. He noticed Rachel's remnants in the car: Chap Stick, a meditation CD, her yoga mat in the back seat. Maybe she was setting the table now, filling up his glass with beer, putting herbs on his pizza. He thought of what she wore. What she might be thinking of. And he got out of his car, and strode to the ditch.

A Heartless Online Dater

*M*adly since fourteen, or wishing to be madly, or, as I've grown older, just madly wanting it, with someone. Usually after being without for a time, and I can sense the width of his shoulders, the muscle of his legs, the way he might kiss my neck. I'd never slut-shame; I need touch like any other, but hese last weeks since my heartbreak, they might have been close to what some call "loose." As for my heartbreak, I won't bore you with him. My bestie would disown me if I did. Still, I'd be lying if I said I don't want him to call. I can't stop hoping he'll come by for the stuff he left or show up at my work with flowers. I take the risk, in relaying all this, of sounding like one of those everything's-all-about-me kind of girls. But I can't change who I am.

I had returned to Minneapolis after being home in South Dakota for New Year's. My parents and brothers and their wives and kids enjoyed a wholesome weekend with food and Welch's sparkling juices and board games while I texted with a redhead from the dating website. He sent funny memes from Nebraska and I sent pictures of the puppy my sister and her husband had just gotten. He was nice, with almost orange hair, and his pictures made him seem like he'd be tall and broad. Normally, I don't date redheads, but it didn't have to be long-term. So Jeffrey, his name, was in the hole when I showed up an hour late. I know that's bad, but I'd just gotten back from South Dakota, and my roommate was in the shower, and I couldn't find the top I was going to wear, and my dad kept calling. Jeffrey didn't care, at least he didn't show it.

"You know," he said from his driveway in his dumpy suburbs. I was walking toward him. "When a girl's on time that usually means she isn't very interesting. When she's fifteen minutes late, she might be okay. But if she's this late, man, she's got to be amazing."

I was laughing too much, then hugging him too tightly for a first greeting, and when we got to the townie bar I drank a lot. It was trivia night and Jeffrey answered the questions by whispering them in my ear.

"Okay," he said, brushing my earlobe with his lips. "If I get all of these right, we're going to have to make out." He got half of the questions wrong, but I didn't stop him when he said, "Niiiice, got every one."

After more drinks, back at his car, he opened the passenger door, and I told him, and it was true, a man had never done that for me. Almost thirty and that had never happened. I tried to think of a time when my heartbreak did, but I couldn't. At Jeffrey's, more drinks, and I couldn't stop making comparisons. He wasn't as tall or as broad as his pictures made him seem, and he had a bad habit of cutting me off mid-sentence. We pretended to watch a movie for ten minutes before we went to his room, and there all I could think of was how he smelled, different than my heartbreak, not as manly. Afterward I could tell Jeffrey was headed to that place men go. His eyes with that glazed look.

"You should stay," he said, all sleepy. "Stay, and in the morning we'll get pancakes at the Original Pancake House." He said, unironically, that it was his favorite spot.

"No no," I said, as I searched for my shirt in the dark, "I should go. Call me, though, okay?" I patted him on the chest. He didn't fight sleep.

In the rush to leave I forgot my bra. I couldn't go back. At home I took a shower and went straight to bed, breathing in my pillow, which held the faintest smell of my heartbreak. Jeffrey texted the next day, saying he had bought me a gift. He was in his mid-thirties and he worked at a bookstore. If he didn't know why we weren't right for each other, I didn't want to go through the process of explaining.

I had another date that night, with a Jewish boy who was cocky, and probably wealthy, if he had filled out his profile honestly. Dinner was his offer, and though I don't like dinner on a first date, I agreed. There I was, waiting in the lobby, and when the Jewish boy arrived I greeted him brightly, with my best smile, wearing red lipstick, showing just the tiniest bit of cleavage. I looked like a catch. He just stood there, hands in his pockets.

"Hey," he said, then looked away. "How are you?"

"Fine," I said, bitchily. But come on, what the fuck?

Things improved somewhat. He talked about himself, even while eating: he engineered bridges, traveled thirty weeks of the year, just got back from Colorado for a ski trip. He might have asked three questions, and I might have smiled twice, which I considered a success. Before we finished our meal we did play footsie, and he gave me eyes like he wanted something. So in the parking lot we made out, but I demurred when he asked me to his place.

"Thanks for dinner," I said, beginning a hurried walk to my car. I barely heard him say, "No problem."

In my dark car I took a moment to assess. I had worn my best date outfit, and my hair was on point. I looked rested. I wished, seeing the best representation of myself in my pull-down mirror, that my heartbreak could see me. On the drive home, Jeffrey texted again. I wondered about my heartbreak, if he was with someone. I cried myself to sleep.

The next day Jeffrey texted again, asking if I'd given up, while the Jewish boy asked if I wanted to go to a club I'd never heard of. I told him I had plans. I told Jeffrey nothing. That night was a date with a boy I'd call "granola." In his pictures online he wore a straw hat in a mystical-looking garden. When he said, maybe as a joke, that he ate what he found in dumpsters, I tried to look past it. He said he'd cook for me, and I assumed funny business.

When I showed up to his house, first thing I noticed was the political signs in the windows. I wore a skirt and heels and a cute top, and the look was not appropriate. At the front door a guy wearing overalls and a hemp parka gave me an eyebrow raise, then turned without speaking, and a hairy dog dotingly followed him down the hallway and out of sight.

I was supposed to figure it out from there, I guessed, so I went up the stairs, which creaked as I walked, and sitting on a ratty couch was a beautiful girl, maybe nineteen or twenty, with her hair shaved on side. She nodded in the direction of the kitchen. Others had come over for the same kind of night. I ignored this uncomfortable truth as Anders gave me a hug in the kitchen. He smelled like soil and man and I would've let him have me on the table, even with the people watching from the other room. He had perfect hair and the right size arms. I liked him so much that soon I was drinking the beer he and his God knew how many housemates had made. But when we went upstairs, I'll be honest, I thought it'd be better. As he slept I deliberately placed my bra beside my jeans on his mattress, which lacked a frame or a headboard. I'd remember this time.

I took a nap after work the next night and for supper wanted a substantial meal, since Anders had made a kale-and-beans dish that wasn't enough for a girl with a behind like mine. I went to a bar and ordered a hamburger and fries, hoping no one would come and talk to me. Back at home my roommate and her boyfriend were all cuddled up watching a movie in the living room. I huddled under their blanket and fell asleep. In the morning more texts, and I deleted them all. The previous night had been so cozy I relished the thought of repeating it, rather than coordinating with some man I didn't know, doing some activity I didn't know if I'd like, requiring makeup and the right outfit. I put on my pajamas and selected a stack of movies. My roommate was at her boyfriend's and I ate delivery from my favorite Thai place. I put my computer on my lap, and instead of watching anything, I went to the site like an addict. One of the instant messages came from a guy who'd written a few weeks prior. I had literally not thought of him since, but I must have been getting buzzed from the wine. I noticed nearly the whole bottle was already gone.

I wanted to be distracted from the texts, I think—the ones my heartbreak once sent. Reading them over and over again had become an obsession. Before I knew it an average guy sat beside me on my couch having a drink. I hadn't changed from my pajamas, and he didn't seem to care. He wore khaki pants and a button-up shirt and parted his hair where he was starting to bald. He said he was a sales manager at a retail store.

"You wanna go upstairs?" I asked after we'd talked for twenty minutes. I told him, before we started, that I had to get up early.

The next day, a Saturday, he texted to see if I wanted to go out. "For real this time." I trashed it, along with others. I responded to Anders, even if we wouldn't see each other again. He didn't have a car, and driving over to his place for roots and berries and a night of sleeping on his floor would be a one-time thing. That afternoon I cleaned my room, did laundry, and in the early evening went to the gym. When I got back my roommate told me she and her boyfriend were planning to go out. No one I had met the previous week stood out enough to call and give false hope to, so I went with them. My roommate's boyfriend drove us and we got drunk, and soon two boys had joined us in our booth: one bald completely, the other with a shaved head but balding too. The one with the shaved head was quieter, with blue eyes, and he said he was a writer, which I thought was ridiculous since he had never been published. The other was a schoolteacher and gregarious, and even if I would've liked the writer more, it wouldn't have mattered. The schoolteacher was so forward.

As it became clear I'd leave with them, I felt my roommate kick me under the table. She was jealous. She's been with her boyfriend for three years and has begun to disappear to other men, like her shared existence is making her invisible. She could be as mad as she wanted to be; I went home with the writer and the schoolteacher, and in the morning I didn't ask for the schoolteacher's number and he didn't ask for mine. He gave me money for a cab and I left. That's what I remember about him, money for a cab, and back hair, and large testicles.

When I got back my roommate and her boyfriend were lazing around, eating their usual Sunday brunch, watching news shows. I could tell by the way she looked at me she thought I was a slut, but I gave her the details, as I knew she'd want them. When she seemed satisfied I trudged up to my room, dizzy, and went to sleep. Sometime in the afternoon I woke craving a long shower. I had another date that evening. I knew my roommate would give me the third degree, and so I left without telling her that I was meeting a guy for pho. My stomach had not settled from the night before. A warm meal would be good.

A PhD student in sociology, the new prospect told me during our online chats that he was in the process of completing his doctoral dissertation on the effects of religion on the right-wing political movement. I lean left, so I thought he'd be interesting. And he was, I'd say, interesting, though he kept biting his lip as if worried about saying something wrong. He had a striking face, though, and I liked, as we talked, imagining being a college student in my late teens, having him as a teacher, falling in love with his bone structure.

"I live close by," he said as we walked to our cars. The sun was setting. He had green eyes. "You wanna watch a movie or something?"

"We could do that," I said, and I went to his place, with its exposed brick and rows of books on wooden shelves. The sex was fine.

The next night was a date with a boy who worked at a grocery store, the one people go to for their organic shrimp and gluten-free pizza. Judging by his pictures, I feared he might be skinnier than I, but I had never been on a date with someone who had so many tattoos or was in a real band. His was called the Black Blues. We met at a bar and right away I was taken aback by how thin he was, more so than in his photos online. Taller, too, with floppy hair and a knit hat tilted back on his head. He had a key chain on his belt loop, and even carried in a bike helmet. As we drank our second beers I noticed a Mancala board tattooed on his forearm. Some of the holes had been filled in, so I asked.

"Each hole represents an achievement in my life," he said.

"So what does that one mean?" I touched one of the filled-in holes.

"That's personal," he said. His name was Evan, though he said he was born a Jason.

"So you changed your name?" I asked later. I was buzzed. "Like, legally?"

"Just never felt like a Jason."

And that's when I realized it was all a mistake. That night definitely, and all the others too. But that's how you get over someone, right? You fill your life in until time has done its job. So even though Evan-Jason and I had no connection, I went with him to a late movie at a nearby independent theater, and though it was a movie about the end of the world, in which the earth gets hit by a giant meteor and everyone dies, I went down on him, and he finished in my mouth.

The next three nights were a blur. I went to an art gallery with a bisexual guy with curly hair who spoke with a lisp, and we had anal in his depressingly bare apartment. I blame the mushrooms he gave me for my blasé attitude, saying something about how I wanted to explore the boundaries of human connection. The night after was Terry, who of all the guys from the last two weeks would be the one I wished I had not met. He had a good job and wore brown-framed glasses, but I must've been too big, or loud, or thirsty, because he never called back. The night after was a guy who lived downtown and told me up front that he was looking for casual sex. In the morning I had a hard time remembering where I'd parked. The night after was a Christian who said he lived in a "living, breathing community," whatever that meant, and I shouldn't have let him sleep over because now my pillow smells more like his Axe cologne than my heartbreak. Then it was Saturday night, the night I did the worst thing. I called Jeffrey and told him that things had been really busy and I'd make it up to him by cooking dinner. He came over and I got my bra back, but I haven't replied to his texts since.

Now it's later, and all I can think about is another. I know I should slow down and "center myself." I need to "love myself before someone will love me." But those are just words people use to make themselves feel superior to those who don't have anyone. I can't stop thinking about him.

Cheater

Those who really knew Steven Johnson would agree his wildest times were behind him, back in Ohio where he fulfilled his military duty. Those years are now a drizzly tour of youth: musty strip clubs, dank basements for playing drinking games with fellow airmen, tidy apartments of twentysomething blondes with well-paying jobs in public relations.

Steven still parts his hair straight down the middle, like he did in the Air Force, and when he speaks he tilts his head boyishly. It's one of the mannerisms that originally charmed his wife, Polly. Light beer is his favorite drink, though he likes rum at parties and diet sodas when golfing, one after another as if they were water itself. Every other day he exercises on a stationary bike, even on days when Polly tells him to skip it so they can go out and see a performance of a play written by Polly's friend who attended Carleton with her but now is living in Tacoma. Though even if Steven misses those nights, he doesn't forget to tell Polly he loves her, and she tells him she loves him. So it has to be that, what they call love.

As for work, Steven spends his days as a computer engineer in Seattle. He has a friend named George, who works for a package delivery company as a dispatch supervisor in the nearby industrial district. The two of them go golfing almost every Saturday, but Steven likes the game more than George, enough that he'll go to the driving range on his lunch breaks. Boeing, known for constructing planes and defense systems, lets him take as long a lunch break as he pleases, provided he gets all his work done. Often Steven brings his secure laptop to bed, which Polly hates. She believes it distracts him from the things they could be doing, like staying out at George and Nina's, drinking IPAs and eating hummus and playing cards. Polly doesn't really like hummus, or IPAs, or even cards, she likes going there because George and Nina help her feel better about her relationship with Steven. George and Nina are never sneaking kisses or cuddling like she and Steven do. In private, Steven has said to George that Polly is the "most insatiable woman" he's ever met. Even still, through their differences, by the pecks Steven gives Polly on both cheeks after he puts his laptop away but before he puts on his sleeping mask, she knows they'll be together for life.

One clear day in the middle of last summer, Steven and George went golfing. Milling about the first tee box, George looked humble and a bit dense, not as successful or clever as Steven. Still they were good friends, and George thought they always would be. In those good spirits he stretched as Steven went into the clubhouse for refreshments, returning with a diet soda in one hand, a hot dog in the other, and a bag of trail mix sticking out of his shirt pocket. He tucked away the light beers in his golf bag and in his cargo shorts' pockets, like condensing rockets. They swung their clubs to warm up, George using his longest irons while Steven used his driver, over and over, making whooshing noises in the long grass behind the clubhouse in the shade of a tree.

That's when George saw them. Two women in visors and neat, brightly colored shirts, Lycra tights under form-fitting skirts, looking like they'd never known life without the possibility that something good was about to happen. How effortless they seemed, almost out of place among regular humans, making George think—like he always did when he saw forms like theirs—about Nina, his wife. How many times he had seen their own tense gazes reflected in the windows of the vegan restaurants they frequented. How easily he would get obsessed, then, with how silent they were, not talking the way couples do, whispering to one another about the little things no one else cares to hear. Those people, though he never told Nina this, are the ones who are really in love: the ones who kiss for ten seconds when they say goodbye in the morning, as is prescribed by relationship counselors.

No one accompanied the two women swinging drivers by the tee. But who then, George sarcastically thought, would give them permission to tee off? How would they know where to stand over a putt? Would they be judging all these situations without the advisement of a man? George began to hope that he and Steven would be paired up with them.

"Next up," the tee announcer said, "Johnson, party of two, Johnson." The two men walked up. "Afternoon, folks, I'll have you playing with these young ladies over here."

George looked over, and one of them smiled. "Hi," she said, shaking his hand. "I'm Rachel."

"Maria," the other woman said. They crisscrossed, and everyone was introduced, and now it was time to tee off. George went first, and as he placed his tee in the ground he understood that the next moments of his life would be instrumental, crucial to how everything would unravel. He often had these kinds of moments: overseeing a new employee at work, talking to the yoga instructor at the gym, leading the adult group at church, each moment important because of the woman opposite him. This time she had dark straight hair and a white smile and her name was Rachel. The first-tee jitters were always there, strangers assessing the length and height of another man's drive, but this was different. Heart pounding, George coiled his body, eyes intent on the dimpled sphere and swung. The club smacked the ball, and though the drive did not travel on a normal trajectory, staying much closer to the ground, George was happy. It went long and true.

"Nice shot," Rachel said as she strolled up to the tee. She perfunctorily hit a proficient drive. George admired it, relishing the idea of getting used to the way her ball skimmed the ground. Maria hit next, and her stubbier form produced a whip, but her shot went even farther than Rachel's. Steven was last, placing his tee deliberately before stepping away for a few more practice swings. On one, he grounded his club, and George suppressed a laugh. Steven gave a self-admonishing tilt of the head and swung again, and after his slicing drive the two men veered off to the right and into the trees.

"I cannot believe we got paired up with two hotties," George said. He was giddy.

"Come on," Steven said. He took a gulp of beer. His hat was moist around the brim. "They're married."

"Did you see any rings?"

"Doesn't mean they're not married," Steven said, and took another drink. George was too stunned to answer. He hadn't even considered that.

When they convened to putt, George thought it was like a family reunion. For the first time in years he would get to see how everyone had grown. Rachel was tanned and fit, like a hurdler. She wore a Boston Red Sox cap and George could tell she had always been popular. Maybe she came from money. With her history swirling in his head, he made his putt. No one but Rachel noticed.

"That's a birdie?" she asked.

"Can't believe it," George said. He jauntily threw his ball in the air, then caught it on the way down. He rubbed it clean of any debris. After the rest made their putts, their balls plunking into the recessed plastic—all four believers in the sanctity of a true score— they went to the next tee in unspoken communion. Steven cracked open his second beer as the women worked on their firsts. George didn't drink, so he couldn't blame alcohol for his drive hooking badly. The women, not ashamed, laughed like sisters, intimately touching each other's arms and shoulders as they headed toward their errant drives. Steven drank as he walked. The alcohol and sun and camaraderie of sport would be enough to dissolve the group's newness. Only a matter of time, George thought, and they would talk of real things: where they worked, where they lived, who they were seeing. And it took even less time than he expected. On the seventh hole, just two lazy clouds in the blue sky, the sun warmed every part of them, down to their toes in their socks in their brown golfing shoes and up—to the thin strip of their stomachs showing between skirt and top, to the sweating divide between their breasts.

"So are your husbands missing you two today?" George asked Rachel. Maria was a family therapist. Rachel, a physician's assistant.

"Husbands get in the way of golfing, George. We wouldn't want that." And she nudged him with her shoulder, which made George aware of the ring on his finger. It was like a heavy weight. He wanted to throw it in the nearby creek, and if they heard a gentle plop, he'd say, "I don't know. Weird noise, I guess."

Maria and Steven were out of sight in the sand trap, but both Rachel and George heard Steven say, "If you open your stance like this."

"My boyfriend hates golf," Rachel said. The sound of sand being displaced, then giggling. "Hates it. I couldn't drag him out here if my life depended on it."

Maria's balled rolled to rest on the green. George wanted to kick it back in the sand and stride into the nearby lake and submerge himself until he drowned. They walked to the next hole, and he abandoned all hope. There were another nine holes. God only knew how many merciless years.

At the turn they stopped in the clubhouse for more beer, and after their drives on the tenth hole Rachel took off her top. Paces ahead, she unfettered herself down to a spandex bra. George doubled over, sick with lust. Maria stripped down too, showing an equal amount of skin. The men turned to one another, and Steven grinned. George shook his head. At the seventeenth green, clothes back on and the sun's sting lessened, it was once again Rachel and George, Steven and Maria off behind a tree. George heard them but could not make out what they said.

By the final green they knew the names of boyfriend and wives—Maria was the only one without a significant other—and had become comrades, telling galvanizing stories. They were friends, it could be said, and Maria suggested they go to the bar not far from the course. She offered to drive Steven, and Rachel would go with George, who, it turned out, lived only blocks from her. A pragmatic cruelty, was all George could think. At the practice green after all eighteen they took pictures, and George still has them. One with everyone holding a putter, another with each of them putting a hand on the same driver, and one with their arms around each other. Sometimes George looks at the pictures on his aging phone and wonders what life could've been like had he had the courage to ask Rachel out. He hardly knew her, but he believes their life together could have been perfect.

After the photos they went to their cars, spent and red-skinned. Soon they'd put food in their bellies, making the day more satisfying. At least there was always that, George thought. At the grill the drinks had arrived but Steven and Maria had not. When the food came, Rachel made a phone call to her friend. They did not hold hands, though it could be said, at least in that moment, that George and Rachel did share a nervous closeness. He could always say that much, years later when cursing himself for being faithful, thinking of the time he went golfing with the love of his life. He looked over at Rachel listening. She relaxed her shoulders but raised her eyebrows, then she smirked.

Yearning

A sign hangs duct-taped on a steel traffic pole at a busy intersection. Stenciled in bold letters are the words: MEET LOCAL SINGLES. John and Dena pass by it on their way to the bus in the dark early morning in Seattle's Central District. Not so dark that John cannot notice Dena's face. How pale it is. He's always liked that about her. Her alabaster complexion reminds him of the adolescent Goth phases experienced in different parts of the country at roughly the same time in the mid '90s. But her face is not completely white. Two patches on her cheeks glow like the rosy skin of a peach. John and Dena wait for the light to change as John begins to wonder, like he does every morning, if others have something like that sign in their lives: a weird billboard, a drab office building, a crumbling sidewalk, something reminding them that they hate everything about what they have become. They've passed it now. They've walked a block.

"I wonder," John says. "You think anyone calls that number?"

Dena isn't listening, so she doesn't answer, but John doesn't resort to name-calling. Once upon a time, he would have. In their biggest fight, years before, John called Dena "spacey" and disparaged her private school. He waited as she leaned back against the wall, aghast. Each of the next words she said, she said with a pre-meditation John would never shake.

"You know, John, I was with other guys back in my 'bullshit school,' and every one of them lasted longer than you." Then she closed the bedroom door.

Since then, John hasn't brought up her spaciness and Dena hasn't brought up his stamina. Still, John is touchy and will from time to time play the what-are-you-thinking-now game when he sees her looking off. He is positive her dreaminess is founded in nothing deep. The sign fades behind them. He regroups and asks again.

"You think anyone actually calls the number?"

"Huh," Dena says absently, causing his gait to change slightly. She doesn't notice. It's cold on this damp morning. Cars drive by in a haze of glistening brake lights.

"The sign," he says. "The one that says meet local singles, you think anyone ever calls it?"

"I have no idea, John." They keep walking, and at the bus stop they appear like a couple. John is taller, with dyed-black hair, while Dena is fit and nearing thirty-five, with no children and red hair. If a stranger had to guess, these two work in professional settings.

"What time are you getting home?" Dena asks.

"I have to go to the gym tonight," he says. "You shouldn't wait up."

"Do your best," she says, and pats his coat and wheezes out. Hands in his pockets, John looks at others. The younger ones, he wants to catch their eyes, but their attention is on their phones. The schedule has graffiti obscuring half of the day's runs. When the bus arrives John and Dena give each other a kiss on the lips. She gets on and John walks behind in its wake, tasting the strangely appetizing, drug-like fumes. He wipes away a layer of condensation from his phone. He stares at a number he has secretly saved and thinks about calling her until he gets to work, where he finds his chair has been overtaken by his boss.

"Good morning," the boss says. He is bald and rotund.

"Good morning," John says. He finds it comforting to have someone else sitting in that chair. Maybe he is preemptively absolved of the day's errors. Just as John thinks that, his boss stands up.

"Got a lot of extra volume coming in, so we're going to need you to come up with a plan. Mmmk?" The boss pats John on the shoulder, then heads to his larger office. John nods. This is the job: take the shit that comes with allocating packages among a flotilla of trucks so that mostly men, and a handful of women, can deliver them across the southern regions of Seattle. John's lot is not the worst lot. He makes more money than he ever thought he would, even if his concept of how much he would make has stayed the same since boyhood.

"Won't make it until really late. Work, etc.," John texts as Pat flies into the office. She is blonde and wearing brown work gloves and John can smell her through the cold air like manufactured fruit. She is holding a box, breathing heavily.

"I found this out on the end of the belt," she says. Her eyes are wild. "Did someone scan it?" John doesn't look up. "This box," Pat says, as she shoves it across his desk. It hits his hand. "I found it out on the belt and it needs to be scanned or else it's going to show up as an error."

"Well," John says, pushing it back. "Go ahead and scan it." John then pretends to be doing work as Pat stands there. He resists the urge to look up until Pat grabs the package and starts out the door. Before she leaves, she says, "You're never going to move up pulling stuff like this." And the door slams shut and John's phone is buzzing.

"Ride your bike in the morning. I have a surprise tonight."

A surprise. The last time Dena surprised him was with a bowl of soup and after that a full-body massage in the nude. She covered her breasts with oil and slid up and down his back. There had been no occasion. He was just a man with a woman and this was his life. It wasn't until their bedtime routine that he remembered why he was supposed to be unhappy. Dena was brushing her teeth with the organic toothpaste he hated but could never find the nerve to tell her. The smell made him ill.

The morning passes as John clicks, moving digital packages from one truck to the next. He knows that some drivers will say, "You're the best supervisor we've ever had," while others will say he's worthless. Others will have no opinion; they know that whether John is brilliant or a dunce, their trucks will be loaded with more or less the same number and diversity of packages. Everything will always be the same. All life ends in death. When lunch arrives, Pat has forgotten the morning. She has a plate of food.

"Want some?" she offers, beginning to rub John's back with her free hand. She does this with everyone, so John doesn't consider himself special. The kneading gives him tingles down his spine.

"No thanks," John says, seeing the meat and fries and gravy stacked on her plate, looking like the entrails of an animal.

"I haven't eaten for days," Pat says. "I mean I haven't *eaten* eaten for days. Suuuuure you don't want any?" She puts it right up to his nose this time.

"No," John says, and soon Pat leaves to eat in another office. A message from Dena comes in.

"What's the deal?" it reads.

John thinks of his job. He'd love one that allowed him to be physical so he wouldn't have to waste hours of his life in pursuit of maintaining an average shape. Better yet, to live hundreds of years ago, when every person was required to be in shape since everything they did—from getting water to acquiring heat to getting in contact with a friend a mile down the road—took effort. There was no gym membership. Gym membership cards were punched at birth.

"Yes," he writes, "I'll be there," deciding it best to skip the gym and avoid an argument. John leaves for lunch. He eats a sandwich from the vending machine in the break room alone, staring at the number.

Months before, John was at a house Dena dubbed the "Hot House" because of the young women who flowed in and out.. Gary lived there. The two met via an intramural Frisbee team, and became friends after a couple weeks, finding they both loved Russian literature and black-and-white photography and making fun of those who listed *The Matrix* as the only film that mattered in the last twenty years. In Seattle, it wasn't that hard to find a guy like Gary; for most it wouldn't be, at least. John had always had difficulty making friends. So it was a miracle to find Gary, but it was some kind of cosmic one-off that Gary lived with the women he lived with, who all worked at the same nonprofit building houses and had the same lithe body and unkempt hair. John loved going to Gary's. The young adults there listened to John's stories about how it was good to avoid the rat race of society, and how he used to write for *Pitchfork*, "back when it was still reputable," and how he once wrote a novel but nothing had come of it "yet."

On that same night months ago, after John danced to rap music that he, unlike everyone else at the party, didn't know, after he smoked weed on the porch and ended up in the kitchen and talked with the just-out-of-college kids until the morning, close to the time when he would have retired on the couch, she walked through the door. One man held her right hand and another her left. A squeal, and one of the other girls from the house ran up and they all four jumped up and down and hugged and kissed. John was taken for the thousandth time. A small coil of hair wrapped around her ear, she brushed it back as she laughed. He saw her radiate. John lost track of time and now she was right in front of him, saying, "Hey, big guy, you're a better door than a window."

"This is John, the door," Gary said, giving his friend a sloppy pat on the shoulder, and it was then that passive John—a description he didn't like but knew it applied to him—decided to say, "You, my little bird, are beautiful."

Now Pat flies into the communal office.

"I'm going," she says, one purse slung over one shoulder and another draped the other way, making a cross on her chest. "Marc said I could go home early."

"Oh," John says without looking at her

"I've got a softball game and I'm always staying late, so I'm going." Pat slams the door, leaving John to wonder if the weight-loss pills she says she takes make her the way she is. But Pat has always been erratic and will always be and the only way out for John would be to leave. This is something he tells others he might actually do, but he has no real intentions. Quiet in the office now, John locks the door. In the silence he is left to complete his tasks.

"Hurrying, baby," he messages. "Can't wait to see the surprise." But John doesn't hurry. Instead he goes online and reads news stories and spends more time gazing at the number.

Work ends, and John is already late but he decides to walk home. He'll get exercise and be more at ease for the surprise, he reasons. He walks in the cold of early spring. Dark again as he passes the park where they have sat for hours, reading in the sunshine, Dena wearing her bikini. Many times over the years John has caught guys looking at her memorable figure. In the distance now emerges the outline of the downtown buildings. On their third date John took Dena not to the Columbia Tower but to a significant building in its own right, and she told him, "A boy who takes a girl to a place like this is only looking for one thing." They laughed about it the next morning, the newness of their naked bodies. Closer to home, on the sidewalk where he and Dena have taken many walks, he thinks about the last one, on Sunday. Dena was telling him about a new guy at work who made her laugh "really hard" when John thought he heard a noise.

"There's a baby crying," he said, but she never heard it.

Faith

That summer of their junior year he declared his intention to guard her heart; soon, he wondered, would he be able to call her his girlfriend? She'd be going into her last year of college before veterinary school. She loved horses and wore a belly-button ring and listened to Five Iron Frenzy. She tickled people in vulnerable positions, like when they were driving. But when she stopped answering David's texts after that galvanizing evening of praise of worship songs in her parents' basement, he began to doubt, and when she stopped replying to his emails and they went on to their first jobs on opposite sides of the country, he found that he could not locate, within his whole mortal body, one single cell that believed in God.

Astronomy

And so while it seemed when Lacey broke up with David at the beginning of his senior year that it would be the end of the world, the earth kept spinning. If anyone had bothered to measure all the science on that day of David's personal record for emotion stirring in his soul, they would have found it to be a regular day: the sun precisely 92.96 million miles away, the moon at exactly 238,900 miles, with the axis of the earth oscillating with perfect obliquity between 22.1 and 24.5 degrees. But all that was too between-the-ears, too academic and not enough of the heart and loins, with which Lacey and David were concerned in their brief three months together, over a summer of trading head rubs on an island near a Christian camp, holding hands on a plane ride to Winnipeg, and making out on the plush downstairs couch in David's parents' house as the credits for *The Shawshank Redemption* rolled.

King of Israel

What can you do in that situation, with a rudderless son who shaves his head—though he appears to have plenty of hair—and cries when his car breaks down, and who majored in psychology, though he said he doesn't want to teach, or work in any field relating to psychology. Mostly the boy collects CDs and dreams of having a girlfriend. Outside the sun was setting, the smell of spring, the apartment very still, there in the year after he graduated from college David talked with his dad about the rest of life. A son who worked as an in-school suspension supervisor in Sioux City. He carpooled with women twice his age. He made spreadsheets of the Christian albums he needed to own. Two years later on a cold frozen plain in Sioux Falls, David was destroyed by a Nebraskan volleyball player. Just a week after that he met an Alabamian on MySpace, and like David he was tempted and failed once more.

Rented Room

His name is James Nelson and hers is Betsy Brownstein. Their bodies are touching. Breathe in the remains of last night: alcohol, cigarettes, sex.

"She's my best friend," Betsy says. "We talk every morning. I call her or she calls me, it's cute, isn't it?"

James does not say if it is cute or not. He takes Betsy's fingers and taps them on his chest like a drumbeat. She speaks with her friend for several more minutes. He has fallen in love.

Weeks before, on a quiet night, James was alone in the house where he rents the upstairs. For years he has scraped by, working odd jobs while trying to make his photography full-time. His photos have appeared in marginally distributed national magazines, and the taste of those tiny morsels of his dreams has caused James to consider moving to New York, though never seriously enough that he actually makes any plans. In the hush of his rented quarters, James read the messages he had received from this Betsy girl so far. Swiping the screen of his phone, he loved that she was curly-haired and mentioned "deals" in her profile. James admired her dimples. He allowed his hopes to rise. He had written to Betsy days before, a message about the deals he'd procured at a secondhand-clothing store. As he watched football that Sunday afternoon, what started off as "Why the heck not?" grew into a "Could this be something?" The announcers discussed a possible overturned touchdown, and James's thoughts went: "She's funny. I wonder if she's as pretty as her pictures."

And she gave him her number. Imagine the texts. Betsy, twenty-three, back from Thailand on a Fulbright Scholarship: her digital self alone made James different. His coworkers at his day job noticed the way he carried himself: "The Natural Evolution of Betsy Brownstein and James Nelson by way of Texting in 2012" is what they might have called it. From trivial details of their profiles to flirtations concerning her backside, these messages James Nelson will always remember.

"I don't know how to tell you this," Betsy wrote one afternoon. "But I kind of have a big ass."

James was at work when he read it, and he almost had to hide his phone out of sheer excitement. They spoke once before their first date. James drove away from work that night unworried about what Betsy was doing or who she could be doing it with; whatever it was, it was her business, and it could never be as good as what they would have. At home, James texted, "Just, like, talk...on the phone?"

"LOL," she replied. "Sure." Betsy was laughing when she picked up, and for hours neither feigned the need to leave. It ended because they were exhausted. "I like getting a full eight hours," she said before they hung up.

"What a healthy girl," James thought, "what a wonderfully healthy girl." And he slept soundly, falling into dreams while shaping, based on the few pictures, a large round behind.

James arrived first on the cold December evening, choosing a booth away from the front, where the wind whistled in and could disrupt their time. He sat near the back with the jukebox and ordered a beer and pumped himself up: This will not end with heartache, he thought. But their first greeting was inauspicious. Betsy went for a hug and James reached out for a handshake. They corrected and did an awkward combination of the two. James apologized before they even got settled.

"That was weak," he said. "I can do better."

"I'm sure you give great hugs," Betsy said, taking off her scarf, appearing as a transposition of her photographs: energetic eyes, curly hair, dimples. She could see him staring at her. "So, do I look better than my pictures?"

"Maybe," James said, doing his best laid-back impression, but that's all it could ever be. They ordered drinks and started on about who they had seen from the website. Betsy spoke jokingly until she came to a Minnesotan who worked at NPR and fished in the winter and had wrestled in high school. She spoke with more reverence about him. James noticed and wrapped his scarf around Betsy's neck.

"This smells good," she said, and they started to play a game where one squeezed the other's knee under the table. Later, she wanted James to touch her butt.

"Real quick." Betsy half stood, and positioned herself in the booth. James took a look around the bar before he reached across for a handful.

"What's the verdict?" she said.

"Couldn't say," he said, settling back in his seat. "That wasn't enough." And that exasperated her, the way James said it.

"I'm going to the ladies' to recover," she said, walking away slowly so he could look. He considered her shape to be life itself.

When she got back he paid, and they left. On the sidewalk she hooked her arm into his, attaching her fragile body. "Hold on, Betsy," James said. "We're almost there." As if sailing on the ocean, he would protect her from the tumults. In his car James turned on her seat warmer. That convenience made them closer. "I've wanted to do this all night," he said, and it was like some kind of dream coming true, for James Nelson to kiss Betsy Brownstein. He wanted to be a photographer, but he wanted to be in love more.

"Let's go back," Betsy said before long. She lived close, so James drove, parking on the street where Betsy's brother and sister-in-law lived.

"Now you can see how good it is," Betsy said, taking off her skinny jeans. He took in her impossibly small underwear. He grasped her backside as they began to make out.

"That's nice," he said in her ear. "Really nice."

Later, Betsy glided on top of him in the back seat, and her giggling—which, she'd said in the front seat between kisses, "all guys loved"—went silent. They reached their end. He walked her to her door.

"But for real this time," Betsy said at the side of her brother's house. "I need to go."

In his rented room, James's first instinct was to call her. He didn't want to be called a "creeper," but before he knew it he had dialed her number.

"I have to be quiet," she whispered, "my brother's room is across the hall, but you should tell me things."

"Tell you things?" James asked.

"Yeah, the things you wanted to do to me tonight," Betsy said, "if we would've had more room. Tell me things."

So James told her these things, and after he told her everything he could think to tell, they texted. In the morning his phone rested on the pillow and he had a new message.

"Does she make bomb oatmeal cookies?"

"She" was a girl from the website who went by the screen name *PetiteChanteuse*, someone James would not have mentioned to Betsy but felt he needed to in order to keep up. Betsy had told him about a lawyer who she described as boring and a med student who she really needed to end things with soon and a fisherman who also taught wrestling and knew a lot about Colombian politics. Sitting at his desk at work, looking out at the traffic, James could think of nothing to say other than what he believed was the truth.

"I doubt it," he wrote, and by midafternoon they had planned their evening. James would pick Betsy up from her house.

What she wore that night: a red coat, Sorel boots, gloves that could also be mittens, a stocking hat with a dangling pom-pom, James remembers that. The dome light dimmed as she leaned over to kiss him, like a wife doting on a husband—cordial and expected and full of comfortable affection. Betsy held James's hand, the one not on the wheel.

"I know she can't make cookies like these," Betsy said, feeding one to him as he drove. This was right, James thought. This, he deserved.

He bought the drinks at the bar. Betsy had said how poor she was. She had attended the most expensive private school in the state of Minnesota and traveled to Thailand three times, what did it matter, they sat on high stools, his hand over her wool tights. The bar contained a raucous energy. Townies congregated by the stage and a burly man wearing a cowboy hat and tight jeans gyrated his hips behind a woman in even tighter jeans.

"That woman wants to fuuuck," Betsy said, and James laughed. They got tangled in each other. When Betsy's friends showed up they secured a larger table near the stage. Betsy's "bestie" was blonde and tall, with big eyes and lips, someone who, Betsy said, "if she likes you, you're in." James was introduced, though the bestie didn't hang around long, only showing up later to sing a Tom Petty song with Betsy. Betsy sat back down next to James after it was done, and that kind of amazed him, that she would decide to sit by him. He gave her a kiss in her hair.

"You were really good," he said.

"It was bad," Betsy said. It seemed she would cry. She was drunk. So was James.

"No-no, it was really good," he said, and they kissed as a way of making up.

The cab came as Betsy finished her second and last song of the night, "Killing Me Softly," and James was like a bodyguard, rushing her out of the bar into the back seat of the waiting car. The ride home was a blur, except when Betsy, a woman from Connecticut whose grandfather owned several nightclubs in Minneapolis, and the driver, a Somali man who fled his country in 1993, began arguing.

"I lived in Thailand, okay," Betsy said from the back seat. "I lived in Thailand for a year, so all I'm saying is I know what it's like to be away from your family."

James took Betsy and planted one on her mouth to make her stop, and soon enough she faced the back window. How crazy, thought James, all the while batting away another thought, that none of it was crazy at all for Betsy. Back in his quiet upper level, Betsy collapsed on the couch as James went to the kitchen. He returned and fed her saltines and water. In his bedroom later, it could not be said that they broke any records. But there would be many other nights in the sober light, James convinced himself.

Betsy spoke with her best friend in the morning and James played with her slender fingers, their nails painted red. Light came through his window, and more than the mix of dirty laundry and photography equipment, he smelled Betsy. The date with the liberal fisherman loomed, and she had to be getting back. No matter what happened, James convinced himself, nothing would be as good as what they had. That night he went out with friends to a bar known to be populated with the blogging twenty- and thirty-somethings in Minneapolis. James and his people didn't normally patronize the establishment, and he doubted he would have a good time, but he held his head high, carrying with him the memory of Betsy, knowing if she were by his side he'd be welcomed in the places that mattered. Later, a text from her still had not come. James started to worry. When he felt the buzzing and saw her number, all the world's problems evaporated.

"Hey!" he answered in the loud joint, his finger in his ear, "what's up?"

"Hey," Betsy shouted back. "So my friends want to go dancing or whatever, and I think he might be there, so it might be weird if you come? I don't want you guys fighting over me." Betsy's voice was muffled by other voices. "But I should go because I can barely hear. Call me later, okay?"

"Okay," he said, and they hung up. A plow unearthed the contents of James's stomach. A message came right after: "I'm sorry. I do want to hang out. But I wanna see what the fisherman is like drunk and dancing before I make a final decision. Early next week?"

James began to type a reply but stopped, and for a while stood there reading her old messages. His friends drank and talked around him. As he stared into the loud happiness, everything melded into one. He looked spacey, so one of his friends leaned over and asked, "Everything all right?"

"Sure," James said, his eyes jerking back as if he had just been given smelling salts. "But I think I might head out."

This was not new. James's few close friends always told him, "Don't get so ahead of yourself," but each time they did, it seemed, their words went more unheeded than the last. On the drive home, James thought of what he could say. The unjealous texts had to be out there. He just couldn't find them. Back in bed, throwing his phone across the small room was the only thing to do. In the morning James scrambled over to where he'd thrown it. Only a few minutes went by before he gave in.

"Betsy," he wrote, "I want to see you again."

And all afternoon James waited. He went to the gym but left almost as soon as he walked in, not liking being away from the messages she might be sending. He tried to edit old photos, but that was fruitless. He even thought, on several occasions, of going to see her at her work, though each time he thought that he remembered he'd gotten the idea from a movie. In the early evening he decided—even if he knew it was considered a cardinal sin—to send another text.

"How was your night?" he asked, and when her text dinged minutes later it was first a relief, making him slump in the chair he sat in; then came a familiar pang, making him get up and pace.

"Oh," she wrote, "fun. Sweaty."

An hour later and drunk, James sent the words, "Betsy, you're awfully cavalier with love."

A two-screen message was next, and it came with such alacrity it seemed as though Betsy had it saved in her phone for times such as these. "It's just too much, too soon," she wrote at the end.

James called immediately, and Betsy's phone went straight to voicemail. He went to his computer next, and slapped out an email about how he "wasn't trying to get too serious," though even as he pressed send on what was supposed to solve things, James had the feeling that he had made the worst mistake of his life. That night, he slept on the floor.

Work the next day existed in a world superimposed onto another. Matter, physics, all angles had been bent and misshapen. James checked his email often, and when his inbox finally did light up he knew the contents of message, newly pink. The picture of the person who sent it: her curly hair went past her shoulders, and she was smiling, her dimples showing. Betsy Brownstein. James Nelson's bread and salt.

"I'm sorry," her message ended. "I do think you're great, though. Be in touch. Betsy."

James sat back in his chair as the world collapsed into itself. That night, he went to someone he knew, also from the dating website, and tried to forget as she pulled down her spandex work-out pants to reveal that she wore nothing underneath. Her large nipples, the taste of her mouth, her shaved legs, but all James could think of was Betsy. He wished they could have coffee and talk over the things he had done wrong and would never do wrong again. Later that week was worse. James and a friend went to a club they had frequented years before, and the beats of the music and the lights and the young people all reminded him too much of her, of friends of hers, of people who would call on a weekend to do "fun sweaty things." Alone on his mattress, James dreamed he saw Betsy on the dance floor, with the progressive wrestler grinding behind her, slapping her in the face with his penis like a fish flapping on a dry dock.

The familiar weeks and months followed and James thought of the things he would never learn: what her first kiss was like, if she had ever been scared of dying, if her heart had ever been broken. Enough time passed and James stopped thinking of any of that. He stopped trying to convince Betsy they were right for each other and only the things around them had gone wrong. She deleted her profile. He deleted his.

Kiss Me or Whatever

*P*eanut butter, marshmallow fluff, Nutella. Three jars on a table like saccharine towers. Someone must have brought them to the gallery opening and forgotten to bring them home. Now the night before, and across the street he waits. Through the large window of the gallery he sees them drinking, eating small cheeses, and having a great time. The front door opens, and she walks out. Peter's heart flutters, he sits up, and as she approaches he realizes for the first time how unattainable she is. Once considered attractive, Peter is now balding and online dating and working as a manager at a retail store in the Mall of America. When he went in for a brief moment to vie for her attention and see her art, he could not help but be inundated with by the other artists, who were all younger and had thick hair and vintage leather boots whose eyelets came up to the cuff of their tapered pants. She peeks inside his increasingly shabby vehicle, which he once was so proud of.

"So what do you need, Peter?"

Her name is Ariah. They met on a website she joined "on a goof." For her, she said, dating had always been easy. She had recently graduated from a private university in New York that teaches only art. Peter likes her too much for three dates, two make-outs, and one time in bed.

"Just a second," Peter says. "It's nothing serious, really."

Ariah relents, sits in his passenger seat, barely latches the door. Separately but at the same time they think, *Let's get it over with.*

"It won't take long," Peter says as he fiddles with the dome light. He's losing time. "Why won't this turn off," he says. She does not tell him.

"Don't worry about it," Ariah says. "I need to get going."

"Alright," Peter says. He reaches below his seat and pulls up a plastic grocery bag. "I wanted to give you these, in case you'd run out."

She receives the bag, looks in. The contents inspire a sour smile he doesn't misinterpret. A pathetic strain of hopelessness streams down his face. "Thank you," Ariah says. "It's so much, I'll have to take it to work."

Peter wants to give up now, but he continues for what remains of his pride. "Right, so I just wanted to give you those things and see your art but I also wanted to tell you." He steadies himself. "I wanted to tell you how I thought it would've been weird if that time at my place had been the last time I saw you."

Ariah could melt through Peter's passenger door now. "I thought that might be weird, too," she has no choice but to say.

"So that's what I wanted to do," he says. "I wanted to say that. And I wanted to wish you luck."

"That's sweet, Peter, thank you, but you know we might see each other again. I meant what I said in that email. It was the truth."

"I understand," Peter says, and they sit in silence, for only a moment.

"Well," she says, and she holds up the bag. "Thanks."

Peter's heart goes faster, now that they are in their last moments. Knowing how close to the end he is makes him incapable of thinking of anything other than what he thinks to do. Reaches out to shake her hand, and she does the same. Then she leaves, walking across the frozen street, carrying with her the plastic bag.

Last Friday evening: Peter is by himself, feet on the coffee table. He wears new leather boots, which he bought to salve the heartache. The email came in hours ago, though he only sees it now, which surprises him. He's been drinking and watching videos and the whole time refreshing his phone. Peter stops everything to read her words, searching for the parts that might bear good news. He skips to the end.

"…I don't see you staying single for long. Have fun out there. Leon." Leon is his pet name for her. She has always considered her own too feminine.

Peter takes a long drink, stares beyond the television. This goes on for minutes, hours. At some point he goes to his bed. The room is heavy and spinning.

"You kiss good," he texts, from his mattress on the floor.

Nothing in return and he begins to understand, as he passes out, what her email means. They are done. Five or six drinks before, foolishly, it was his hope.

On a Monday before that Peter is alone on his lunch break, at a mall, on a bench outside a clothing store. He eats chicken strips. He checks his email. All morning he spent crafting the words and now he can be seen by shoppers opening and reopening his phone, making sure he has not missed a reply about the movie they "really should see." An elderly couple walks by holding hands. He hopes for that. When his break is over he has to stand up and throw away his waste, and as he puts his phone in his bag, two messages come in. Never can he now forget the phrase "maybe too relationshipy."

Just the afternoon before, Ariah asks him, "Did that feel good?"

Peter's head is resting on her small breasts. The latex is full of his love. Moments before, she asks, "Do you want to do it like this?"

"Yes," he says, so they do, and it is as he imagined. She is too hot to be here with me, he thinks, even as he is inside of her. Before that, she says, "You're such a thoughtful guy," as the first thing he's done is go down on her, and there he finds himself thanking God for the first time in years. Moments before, they grope each other up the stairs. Moments before that she asks, "Is your roommate coming home, should we go upstairs?" They are on the couch and she is on top as Peter kisses her everywhere, as if Ariah could never have enough body for him to kiss. He feels her smooth skin beneath the cotton of her sweatpants she is wearing for their afternoon of vegging out. Minutes before, she walks up the driveway of the house Peter lives in with an old friend who is now his landlord. The humble front lawn is covered in snow, reflecting the sun. They squint as Ariah first reaches out. Her arm is entwined in his as they walk into the house.

Imagine days before, where in his car she tells him, "Thank you so much." Pieces of her curly hair are in his mouth. "You are so nice."

Before, after eating their meal, they sit in his car. "Seat warmers," he says. "Pretty impressive, eh?"

"My ex had those," Ariah says. "But these work fast, my butt's already on fire."

"I can turn it down." Peter reaches over, and when he straightens she is near him. He could sense the busy street behind them. All the brake lights of passing cars. The trunk of a giant tree just outside the passenger window. Inside, the digital neon displays for speed and temperature.

"So," she says. "You should kiss me or whatever."

Before that they dine at a Malaysian restaurant. She sits—he has secured a booth—and Peter is overcome. Ariah wears a scarf, a low-cut blouse, a skirt and tights, but she wrote in her profile, and said on their first date, that she hated getting dressed up. She makes abstract collages and wants to wear sweatpants every day. The restaurant for their second date is small but full of people. The windows are fogged over. Peter tries to listen but cannot get over her outfit. Leon, Ariah, is an artist, they'll talk about that down the road, but for now they have stories of her coworkers. Time moves. He listens to her. Their food is rice and tofu and nearly gone. She's drunk most of her wine. Peter looks across at her and knows she is the most beautiful creature he could be with in this life. *Jesus*, he thinks, *if I don't do something*, so his leg under the table rests against hers. She doesn't recoil, and soon he asks, as he holds her long fingers, "How long does the paint stay on your nails?"

Now, on their first date, how incredible, Peter thinks, to meet someone who laughs like Ariah, with so much warmth. The others from the site were too flighty or coarse and he is sure this will be the last. Either he and Ariah will fall in love, or he'll just delete the thing and forget. He hopes for the former as they eat their pho.

"I like watching garbage TV and being in my sweatpants all day," Ariah says. "I know that sounds ridiculous, but I don't care."

"It doesn't, actually, not at all," Peter says. "It sounds like a great afternoon. You know, I have a big-screen TV, with *all* the channels…"

"Don't you just know how to charm a lady." And Ariah slaps her hand on his. For a second she keeps it there. This is the first time they touch. They finish their soup in the empty restaurant and have no moments of silence filled with awkward glances. She tells him how she doesn't care about money. He talks about his goals to be a musician, and she seems to believe him, even if he's too old to be chasing after dreams. They leave with their fingertips glancing, and it is so electric for Peter it is like he can detect the exact differences in the prints of their skin. In the parking lot they stand by her car under a white streetlamp. The fall before, she tells him, she drove to Minneapolis from the East Coast. Soon, though, she has to meet her friend for bowling.

"Okay, but hold on just one sec," Peter says, then runs away to his car. Ariah waits. When he gets back he is holding a plastic grocery bag.

"I shouldn't do this," he says, trying to keep eye contact. It's hard with Ariah. She's so pretty. "But I'm being honest when I say I wasn't going to give you this if tonight didn't go well. It's just, you seem really nice and I don't want to come on too strong, but, well, here ya go."

He hands it over, and now as Ariah receives the bag she smiles, a smile Peter has already memorized. She opens it slightly and smiles even wider, though she knows she should not. Peter isn't someone she could want for more than a week or two. For now, she's charmed. She loves this kind of stuff. It contrasts with her aura, which she has been told can come off as too serious. Nutella, peanut butter, marshmallow fluff. She can't live without, she says.

Poem #1

two businessmen dressed in black, hunched and scheming
shrill and overworked, wives floating on a glass of wine
my butt hurts from sitting in this coffee shop chair
how do i become a junior high boy writing love notes for a living
tie tyler in a knot, my uncle's name is greg
there is only water and sugar left in my cup
there was overpriced tea before. comment on capitalism
to chicago this weekend. learn about englewood. comment on racism
oh, the white guilt. i am so guilty all the time
how many naked i have seen in my lifetime
line them all up and bite at their ripe butts. a buffet
ham bits and chocolate mousse. chicken wings. ice in the shape of
tiny beads
these tall businessmen have slinky pockets with jangly keys
and they drank milky drinks. the word milky must be here
now i'm all alone
now i'm all alone
if you say it twice like that it can be poetic
i am sick. i am hungry. i am tired.
feed me butts, so i might gain strength again

i wonder where those businessmen went
off to choke kittens to climax?
this turned dark, like the night sky, out camping all by yourself
isn't that just a lovely line?
the song trumpets by jason derulo, a frog inside the stomach of an
owl, the sound at the precise last moment of your life
is it bells? or silence? or trumpets by jason derulo?
how's that for random. how's that for heartbreaking. how's that
threes. that's a thing
can't be here much longer without wanting to go and wait somewhere else so i can wait somewhere else
a couple walking in. one in a fedora and in a fleece. that must mean
something
i wonder if they can hear the wiggle wiggle of my internal organs
it is so hard to see inside my body
now i see a man bun
well
it isn't really a bun. not a croissant either. a hybrid. a ponytail
emerging like a dinosaur emerged from an egg a million years ago
what if a butterfly hadn't flapped its wings, would you be born?
everybody clap their hands
clap clap clap clap clap clap clap clap clap clap clap clap clap clap
clap clap clap clap clap clap
you're clapping to see if i'm right?
so audacious. such hubris. to question a poet. to question art.
question god
He is watching you now
He saw that

Time

After billions of years and the first atom exploded and caused the forming of matter into planets and suns and space, after our world transformed into a sustainable floating globe of water and fire, after plates crushed together like titans and volcanoes oozed like pimples then cooled and made patches of dirt for us to stand upon, where we could settle and touch butts and breathe air and make more of ourselves, after all that we would come to the conclusion that some places are prohibited because we, the walking globs of watery bacteria, said so? We have the authority? Tell an ant it cannot scurry where it wills.

Sexy

She had red hair and wore glasses and worked for Garrison Keillor, and I hope she didn't show him our sexy texts. Oh, who am I kidding? It'd be so much more exciting if she had. Or what if Garrison Keillor himself had taken the photos; how sexy would that be? Someone could write a whole sexy news story for NPR about the time Garrison Keillor was a photographer for my lady's sexy photo shoot. When he took those sexy pics, how he regaled her with tales of lutefisk and the Lutheran pastor having a bit too much wine before the service and those championship State Fair pies. I always loved the outfits either she or Garrison Keillor picked out. Sheer tights and stretchy skirts and American Apparel bodysuits. But even if Garrison Keillor wasn't her photographer, that ass, I was so glad to see it when I opened my sexy flip phone. For a time, it was my very own prairie home companion.

Courting

Before Phoebe asked if he believed, David was always sure he'd have a clear and sure yes to the question of salvation. Having a quick answer on the nature of Christ was the one thing alleviating the worry David's parents felt for their son, who had wandered for almost three years after college, landing in Austin for now. At least they knew where their boy would be going when he died. But as an almond-haired aesthete named Phoebe, maybe twenty-one, stood with her breasts peeking out of a flimsy white top, her toned thighs bulging out of her impossibly short jean shorts, David found himself wondering how, exactly, he would answer the question of the existence of the supernatural without betraying everything about himself. Maybe, he thought, betraying everything about yourself is how you grow. At the very least it was how a guy like him got a girl like Phoebe.

The Future

We are all journalists now, commenting on each other's statuses. Don't ask me how it works as far as money goes, our bellies are full for sure, but there is quite a bit of suicide among people gone insane with anxiety since everyone online now believes themselves a celebrity. The problem is, and maybe you can sense it, if everyone is a celebrity, then no one is. So no one is, except for the few who everyone knows are, which makes the people who aren't more crazy and depressed. Pair that with the fact that we are living in the most sterilized, overpopulated epoch of human history, with any connection our ancestors once enjoyed with the earth severed, and are all now mortally attached to attracting The Presence—whether as a Blogger or an App Maker—and when we don't make it as one of the top in our chosen Online Presence fields we realize we don't have any other skills, well, you can probably see, even from the past, that's a recipe for doom.

Circle of Life

My phone is not ringing because no one is calling me back. No one is calling me back because no one wants me for anything. No one wants me for anything because I am dumb and fat and bald and old. I am dumb and fat and bald and old because of the human aging process and the choices I have made. I made the choices I made because I thought they were the best choices I could make. I thought they were the best choices I could make after I considered my abilities as a person and the consequences my choices would have for others in the world. I considered my abilities as a person because if I reached too far over my head I could be embarrassed, or I could fail, yet still I was embarrassed, and I failed. I thought of the consequences of my choices for others in the world because I didn't want to disappoint my family—though I do disappoint my family—and I didn't want to hurt others, even though I managed to anyway. My phone is not ringing but I am staring at it, hoping it will light up. I am hoping it will light up so I can answer and be given a job. I want to be given a job so I can have a place to go during the day so that at the end of the week I will be given money for going to that place. I want money so I can buy things like food and shelter and clothes. I want food and shelter and clothes so I can more easily stay alive without having to hunt and forage in the wild. I want to stay alive so I can hear my phone ring.

Fools

I suppose I could say we're all adults and we make our own decisions, and Becca couldn't have been so naive. I drove two hours, away from the highest density of single females in the state of Minnesota, out to a place where the most desirable women have three or four babies and live in a farmhouse. Becca had to have known in her heart that I shouldn't have been there. I should have toughed it out in my bedroom alone, taken up a hobby like putting wooden ships into bottles, or become an amateur philatelist, maybe begun fasting and had true hallucinations, anything other than involving another heart to stave off loneliness. But there she was, across from me on the porch in a metal chair, the tip of her cowboy boot touching my leg, a woman who I was sure would one day be happy with another man, or a man and three other women, and I was flirting with her and she was flirting with me and I could tell, since the night promised to be a boozy one, we'd end up in bed. I don't think what I did could have impressed her, but she was nice, and when we were done she told me how great I was. The next morning, I woke first. Looking out through a crack in her maroon drapes, through gauzy white curtains, I saw the traffic. She lived just off the highway in one of those places you drive by

64

and wonder who lives there. Becca woke, and first thing she did was kiss me, and I wanted to wipe it off. I left after breakfast at a diner, messaging her once, when I got back to Minneapolis. After that I said nothing, but I don't think Becca in western Minnesota, smelling of wild berry, vanilla, and toasted oak, acting in community theater, wearing flowers in her hair, ever thought we'd be something. I say that and I can mean it and maybe I'm right. But there's a chance I'm not.

Premonitions

"That's my diary," she said and snatched it up, hastily putting it away in a drawer with her delicate underwear, many of them so small they served no practical purpose, unless arousal can be considered practical, which I guess it should be, as it leads to procreation, and that's how every single one of us got here. We tried to go to bed afterward, but I couldn't sleep. I could not stop thinking about her diary and what was in it, as if every man—all of them better than I, fitter, with more hair and more possibility and never bound for work at a steelyard—would come to life from the pages and suffocate me in my sleep by wrapping their giant members around my neck.

Affirmations

*E*very social media user loves me. I am the commander of ships. I can write. My mind is brilliant. I am lucky to have been heartbroken. All the ones with athletic backsides who went ghost were level-twelve spellcasters, and I am free of their wizardry.

I believe in our Lord. He wants the best for me. Everyone who accepts His sacrifice and resurrection will live forever perfectly. The numbers 8, 35, and 68 are not unlucky. I have nothing to fear if I drive at those speeds. My tires will not fall off. I am not bad to look at. The hair on my head is as thick as it was at eighteen. There are no lines on my face. I have the waist of a young boy. I cannot get sick. I have never been tired or needed to sleep more than nine hours to feel refreshed in the morning. I do not ever yearn for the buns of those at my exercise class who wear tight shorts and whose breasts glisten with sweat. I do not even think of them. My body is becoming more lithe. It only got thick and sagging because of my lack of faith in our Lord. But my faith has returned and all His gifts are being awarded to me again. My calves are no longer a burden. They do not cause me to lose blood supply when I run more than eight hundred meters. I can jump as high as a basketball player, if I choose. My right thigh is not numb. It does not feel weird when I run my hand over it. The nerves in my back are not pinched from working at the steel factory. You are free of the steel factory.

Testosterone does not make you bald. You are a virile lover. You have made many women come. They are still coming right now. You are a master. Everything in the bedroom is easy for you. You could do it at any time. Never have you left the lofted bed of a dorm room with your pants around your ankles because you were afraid. Shoot your seed. Our Lord will decide if it is right to bloom in the womb. You are capable of rhyming at any time. You never again need to worry about looking at naked women on the internet and masturbating to their nude forms. Doing so will not cause the Lord to punish you by making you go bald.

You have no urge to write about your failures. Social media is a great place for you and every time you log on you receive a flood of notifications. It is no longer necessary for you to log all of your experiences in a document and then for years edit that document until your experiences are shaped enough that you can call it a novel. You never need to write another. You are capable of making great sums of money by becoming a manager. Everyone listens to you. All of your friends love you and want to buy your books. Your books have not sold because they have been suppressed by a secret society hell-bent on destroying you. Your biorhythms are well-tuned and your fasciae are smooth and relaxed. Your biles do not need draining.

Wealth is yours if you want it. You will live forever in heaven with our Lord. You will always look twenty-three. Your first love will spend years searching for you. She never rejected you. Your second love did not reject you either. She was possessed by the devil. You are a spiritual leader. You can write whenever you want. The words are perfect. You never need to go back and edit them until you hardly recognize what you wrote in the first place. Every journal and creative writing website wants your stories. You are the most popular person on social media. Your third love did not reject you either.

You can read the treble clef on a sheet of music. Your words have reached trillions. You can clear your mind of all other thoughts any time you want. You did a fine job in college. There was no need to switch your major to journalism instead of getting a psychology with a focus on teaching. That degree has served you well with many factory and group home jobs. You do not know disappointment. Your strength is legendary. You believe in our Lord. You have no doubts. Snakes are not dangerous to you.

Virginity

"Oh, I love you, David," she said, and hugged him. "I love you so much." And she nuzzled her head into the fabric of David's collared shirt. Was it a sin to say you loved someone before marriage? Emily wondered this as their sweet embrace ended and she stood in the shadow of her boyfriend's—yes she could say "boyfriend" now—handsome frame. What did it matter; it was done. God would judge Emily someday. For now it felt too good to be loved, and to show love, to see it right in front of her face.

Happiness

H e had on his hat, a red farmer hat his dad never wore, and sunglasses from the time his mother had cataract surgery. He walked out into the lake. "Oh, it's not so bad," he called back to her, though he began clenching as the gentle tide reached his testicles, shrinking them. Julia was frozen in place with water ankle-deep. Nathan strode back through the icy Midwest lake and handed her the sunglasses and hat, kissed her, then dove into the murky depths. How silent it was, the voices of children on the shore a muted murmur. Nathan swam out farther still. When he popped back up into the sun, he saw Julia stationed on the sand, wearing his things. Pride and admiration filled his lungs. He waved, then dove again. Years before, after his band dissolved, Nathan had made a sincere effort as a solo guitarist. Inspired by John Fahey and Arthur Russell—as described in the one interview he'd fielded—he recorded a poorly selling album. When the sad tour in support of it ended, he decided, officially, that music was best left for younger men. Nathan had aged, without really even noticing he had, and become less resolute in trying to fulfill the destiny he was once so sure was his. Now he wanted love, and he swam thinking he might one day find it.

Spooky

*F*or a long time, as David lay in his single bed—orphan boys snoring in bunk beds, farting and masturbating at all hours—he pictured Ryan's family. A pregnant wife nestling, settled after having the problems of the day allayed by a familiar voice. How comforting that must be, how good. Sleep later enveloped David, but in the morning, for the first time in his life of sleeping alone, there was an absence next to him, like a ghost, a phantom he did not yet know.

Composites

She was from Alabama and had shining auburn hair, a square pert face, and the kind of white smile that said, "Blow job first, my sweet, then I will go and make us the most hearty breakfast in nothing but my yoga pants." She was the kind of girl they, they being the big corporate fat cats, make up to entice armies to buy their fat cat soap and fat cat French fries. Those fat cats really did a number with her. The very mention of her name was enough to send a growing boy right into manhood. She made Lolita seem dry and dusty. She played volleyball and followed Jesus and I didn't understand her backside in those days. She sculpted and smoked weed and had the softest tummy. She had curly hair and spoke with an accent and asked about my plans. She had grown up in the Middle East and had an overwhelming bosom and loved the films I loved. She painted and laughed a laugh I seldom heard. She came from the coast and did not know how she crushed me. She was Jewish and thanked me each time we kissed. She studied to be a lawyer and had a gap between her front teeth and always giggled. She went to a private college and had an ass so round it hurts to think of. She wore big glasses and came over our first night and told me I was doing well. She taught sociology and texted to say I had been amazing, even wonderful. She was just out of school, or just going in. She had red hair, or a deep brown. She had tattoos, or none at all; her skin is still perfect. She shaved everything, or she let it grow. She laughed, or was always very serious. She came each time we touched, or she never did. But I don't know a thing about her.

Quotes

I want to subsist on the money my small yet supportive publisher sends me. I want to live in the woods, with waves of old flames sending me letters they hid from their husbands about how proud they are of my "continued growth," and "it's really too bad things didn't work out between us." I want one of them to visit because she was "nearby at this conference thing," and when she comes I want the weather to turn bad so we have to wait it out by turning on an old movie we used to watch but never made it to the end. I want her to remember the sensitive way she said I kissed her, and before she leaves, to have a quiet moment at the door. Then for her to be clouded with visions of being an artist's wife, and for years after, while she washes the dishes or vacuums the carpet or wipes the noses of one of her children, I want her to stop and dream about how things could have been, if only they were "a little bit different."

Hall of Fame

The digital screen announced it, appearing while David Martos waited for his order: Bert Blyleven had finally made it into the Hall of Fame. David would always remember, when standing in line for another cheap stopgap for his hunger, that very spot where he learned his favorite baseball player had been inducted. It was a long time coming for the ballplayer, whom David could recall watching on television in his parents' comfortable basement in the summers of his youth. He was a player David always wished would make it, as he seemed to represent the same struggles: hard-working and talented, but always misunderstood and overlooked. But David was none of those things, and he would have realized that if he had realized anything his entire life. Poor, poor, sensitive David Martos, who never got what he thought he deserved, and who never did enough to deserve anything.

Courting

What would Ignatius Reilly say now? Was the wheel of fortune never spinning in his direction? Would Holden Caulfield have news of the phonies? Were they all pitting themselves against the one true man who must wait, like a monk, for his Godly wife? Would Alexandra Bergson do something inspiring, like plant a garden and start living off the land? If David struck out on his own, like her, would Mary see his worth in full as a man? Or how about Howard Roark? Surely he would speak to David now in his time of need, give a long speech on the importance of having value and projecting that value onto mates, never worry about the next one to come along because they come like the next meal or the air. Horselover Fat was the last one David thought of, since he connected with that character the most. What would Horselover do now? Shoot himself and be born again as a new being in an alternative universe? In that place, machines are self-perpetuating hallucinogens and Godly girls with big breasts never have lecherous ex-boyfriends, like they always did in real life.

The End

Near the end of David's final move, after he put down a cardboard box full of things he never used but always felt compelled to take with him, he took a look at himself. A full-length mirror hung on the door, and he could see his blue eyes highlighted by long, delicate eyelashes. It must have been in David's early twenties that a waitress told him he had the most beautiful eyes she had ever seen. David took the pill bottle from the box.

The Bro Novelist

As a man who owns boxes and curates WODs, I have a large social media following. I follow about a hundred people, and have, at last count, over four hundred thousand followers. In my pictures is my small dog, back when it was an even tinier puppy, acting as a juxtaposition to my manly frame. I have several pictures, in progressive stages, of a tattoo taking form on my body, with light streaming into the studio to make sure you know it's not a dingy basement tattoo parlor. I have other posts showing what I eat: bran or quinoa smoothies, on my cheat days a juicy hamburger. I have pictures of mugs that show how much I could never live without coffee. There are the videos of me at the box, set to popular music, with my WOD on the chalkboard, me and a host of fit women wearing our Rogue workout gear. There are the ones at a beach, or at an Animal Collective show, drinking a beer, because we deserve it, followed by a post early the next morning hashtagged with #riseandgrind, to show I'm working out again, earlier and harder than anyone else owning boxes and being rich.

On the plane to AWP, the writers conference, yes, as that is my new goal in life, to be a known novelist, I pulled up a post by one of the few people I follow, a striking Iranian woman who lives in Venice Beach and is American now, I assume, as I've seen every inch of her, down to her mons pubis and all of her backside except for the very middle. She posted like a legend today. From her Bakasana she jumped out to plank, then right into Chaturanga and upward dog. I was surprised that the video passed the terms and conditions, when the end was enough to make them blush in Rio. Her teal swimsuit, I can't imagine it could have cost more than a couple cents in raw materials. When she went into that upward dog I was floored. Her ass jiggled and her thighs like tree trunks led up to such substantial hams from years of burpees and front squats and double-unders. I almost took my leave to go to the first-class bathroom, but *no*, I thought, *this is no longer what I crave*. I needed to set my sights on lithe prizes, marginally in-shape young things just out of college who posted pictures of the covers of Victorian novels beside, not a smoothie after a Bear Complex, but a soda and Jack Daniels after reading and masturbating all afternoon.

"Attendants please prepare for landing," the pilot mumbled through the intercom. We were headed for Minneapolis, with its frigid salt-bleached streets. If Chicago is the somber city, then Minneapolis is the rambunctious younger sister, bundled up in winter gear and ready to put her tongue on any pole. Nowhere else can a man get so much pleasure and the next day have that special snowflake be gone like a snowdrift over its highways, come and come and gone. I retrieved my leather weekend bag from the overhead bin and set out to my hotel, where I could peruse the promotional brochure for the conference. In the airy hallways of my opulent accommodations, I spotted a young woman in supreme condition. We locked eyes, and I could have taken her to one of the alcoves and we could have had our ways, but I didn't want that. I wanted bubbly imperfection, overflowing tits, and hairy thickets, raised on Plath and Wolfe. I wanted her to scream my name then to threaten to kill herself the next day for no reason. The woman I passed never had a day of mental instability. She was hopped up on too many endorphins and lean fish meals; she might even follow me on Instagram. She could send me nudes whenever she liked. We passed and looked back at each other, but nothing came of the encounter, even if she did beckon me with her finger from the closing elevator.

In the penthouse suite drinking high-end Scotch from the minibar, a light snow falling, I looked out at the city, my manicured ab hair trailing down from my bellybutton to my totally shaved pubic area—the rest of me waxed completely except for my beard, which I keep epic—and sort of, I have to be real, I longed to be in one of those apartment buildings in the distance. They must be out there, I thought, greeting friends in from Chicago or Brooklyn who had taken an Uber from the airport. They were now hugging and kissing on the cheeks. So happy to see each other, inhaling missed scents, telling their bestie they have two bottles of wine, handing them a glass already, and "the rest we'll save for after we go out," to a local haunt where they'll meet up with others, even quasi-famous writers, and after coming home one of them will take out a bump of cocaine, then they'll be dancing with the guys they picked up, to LCD Soundsystem and Backstreet Boys, the wine spilling as they go to bed with each other, tearing off the sheer wool tights and t-shirts and getting in deep with just a candle as their light, enough so they can see the good parts but dark enough that the rest is left to the imagination. And what imaginations the young novelists and short-story writers and poets have out there, in all that cold and all that dark. God is not judging them for carnal lusts. God is not judging anything. Rogue is as close to a God as I have.

The penthouse suite was as far away from those creatives as I could be, and that seemed like a curse at that moment. My phone said Liquor Lyle's was somewhere to be seen. I thought to take a car service there and sidle up to the bar and wait for them to approach. I'd stick out in my tailored suit and chiseled body, the rest in their frumpy stocking hats and three-week stubble and muffin-top torsos. And say, "I'm in town for the conference," and they ask if I write, and I have to fib to exaggerate my importance, informing them of my novel that received "decent reviews but no real money."

"Because there's no money in *real* writing," I'll continue, and they might look at me queerly, wondering if I'm feeding them a line. But it won't really matter because we'll soon be here, and she'll be so enthralled with the abs and high ceilings and soft linens, she'll have undressed herself before I even hand her a drink.

Backing away from the window, I took off my complimentary robe and turned on my tablet. The colors, they say, are more vibrant than any other screen you can buy at this size. I scrolled through looking for the videos made by adults who work in retail and live with a girlfriend and have two children, with no lighting or special microphone. The kind of videos where the creator uses his own digital camera to review the latest phone earnestly or recall favorite songs from childhood. The ones where they are cooing in my ear and pretending I am a patient and they are my doctor. I love these videos. They reassure me that there is so much trying in the world. Keep going, they say.

Being driven to the conference in the morning by a man who fled Somalia, I thought about a girl I dated from Connecticut who went to the most expensive private school in Minnesota. Her grandfather owned high-rises in downtown Minneapolis and other properties dotted throughout the country. We saw each other before I got my boxes off the ground. I had moved around the country and dealt with anxiety and paranoia. I could not settle on a place or a job. I was overweight. I lived with an old friend in his attic in the suburbs, and I would have killed myself had I not gotten my Master of Business Administration at night while working at a steel factory during the day and exercising furiously when not working or studying. Either be subsumed in activity or die. I'd have chosen the latter had it not been for working out in a coworker's garage. In that first year, I didn't think I'd ever be able to do even a pull-up, much less a muscle-up, but maybe it was after hauling around so much DOM tube that something changed within me, and all those single-unders accumulated into a double-under greater than myself, and my body transformed. The weight fell off, all the excess lard from years of lonely drinking in forgotten cities.

After so many gains I noticed I wasn't half bad, and I saw myself as I had in college, when I was aloof. Multiple girls wanted to have sex with me when I was a teen, but I didn't understand that; even them sitting on my lap and saying to my face, "I want to fuck you," didn't open my eyes. I was too naïve, too Christian. Years in the future I began to etch a six-pack in a garage, and I quit the job at the steelyard and got my MBA as quickly as possible so I could sell a product instead of being the guy lumbering around like a pack mule for some rich white family from White Bear Lake with five blonde daughters who all wore the same dark-framed glasses and a mom who bore an unfortunate resemblance to Miss Piggy. I did that, and with the help of the guy who ran the box in his garage—he said he no longer had the time—I took over for a nominal fee, and that was the start.

Pretending to have things to do on my phone in the cab with the Somali who spoke in his language to someone else, I thought about the sycophants, the hot young graduates of private schools who don't spell out words in the comments of their articles online but know how to spell in their "real writing." They all loved a new streaming show. I had watched three episodes when it first came out. I watched more episodes last night in the hotel, and I realized this truth: I am old. But I could not resign myself, so I watched another episode, and it got worse. The main character, an Indian born in America, went on a date with a white girl from Brooklyn. They flew to Nashville. They missed the plane back because the comedian playing a comedian wanted barbeque sauce. They also got fake scared over fake ghosts and had awkward encounters with the hotel's front-desk person.

I went online, scrolling madly to find anyone I could commiserate with, but there was not a solitary soul. Then the worst thoughts came, and I worried the conference would be a cesspool of writers and thinkers and content creators all deathly afraid to think anything other than what is perceived to be the most trending opinion, no matter how bad it is at its core. I wanted to tell my cab driver all this, but I had a problem that only the privileged have: I worried about the popularity of a television program wildly praised because it talks clumsily about sexism and racism. All tell and no show, as the cloying writing professors admonish. I am a newbie to this game, I thought as I drifted off to sleep last night, and I need to go in with a positive attitude. Getting close now, the meter ran high. Who cares, I thought, money is not important, only status and power. I am a vessel. Let the right opinions flow through me.

Only once can I remember hearing the gagging noise, and I'm not even sure whether she did that because she had heard guys like the sound or because she actually was struggling to breathe as my prick impinged on her airway, closing the gate of her uvula. Mine is just a tool. Not overly brash and loud like a jackhammer, or powerful and unwieldy like a sledgehammer. Just a hammer. Served its purpose and did the job, sometimes hastily, but completed it all the same.

It may seem like a non sequitur to talk about my prick while standing in the shadow of a brick building in St. Paul where Al Capone would have once smuggled moonshine, the kind of building where they held live flapper shows and there was secret gambling like in a speakeasy and now the ground floor houses a boutique advertising agency, but it's where I am, and I'm having a hard time, stalling, thinking. My Somali cab driver left, and I ended up on the other side of the street watching them all go in. Snow fell and the traffic sloshed up the remains of ice and salt on the sidewalk. Behind me a sliver of an opening between two buildings gave light. For miles I could see, and it should have been bucolic, but looming next to the Prohibition-era building were hearty greetings like a reunion, and I was a long-lost fifth cousin who wanted to horn in on brothers and sisters and fathers and sons and mothers and daughters. Sitting down on a cold bench, I tucked my leather bag inside my Canada Goose. The wet salty snow wasn't good for my Aldens either, and the longer I sat the more rosy my cheeks became. My phone said an Irish bar was pretty close. My glasses frosting, I typed and found a better one about a mile away. I could walk, I thought, clear my head. So that's what I did. I gave up and came upon a stool where I drank craft beers. After my fifth IPA, the last with a meaty aftertaste, I didn't care as much about the networking writers and how many connections they made. But then walked in the hottest babe, "with great tits and an ass to boot." No, sorry, that's for fapping college bros, but "in did walk a fair maiden. Her royal gown…"

I can't stop. I need to tell it like it happened. A girl walked in with her friends, nine or ten of them, I swear. They'd been part of the writing horde, I could tell. I wanted to know everything. "Did you connect with an editor at WhiteCoyote Press? Did anyone show you how to use lit social media more effectively?" I could hear them but could not make out what they said. Their coats on the backs of their chairs, they were ebullient. I ordered another beer. The light afternoon turned to dark evening, snow tranquilly floating to the earth. The neon sign highlighted their descent. Every so often I overhead one of the babes say "Twitter," or the name of an author I had heard of but never read. Mostly they laughed, catching up on sex, I imagined, essential topics friends talk about, not work schedules or the minutiae of inner-office gossip. Their brains worked beyond what made them money.

Perk up, you damn fool. You once dragged yourself up out of obscurity, out of moving around the country, drinking every night, being overweight. You used your own money to go back to school and gain a Master of Business and after that you started a franchise of boxes. You started to be with women who you thought belonged on the cover of movie posters for a sex comedy from the '80s, or a video workout in Hawaii in the '90s. You made yourself into a man who could approach those women, in your Bonobos suit and Warby Parker glasses and Canada Goose coat and Alden boots, and even if you run out of things to talk about, you have tattoos and they have tattoos. They drank shots and wanted company. Get up, go over and ask them their names. So that's what I did, and to my surprise I learned this: they were the twelve apostles and I was the Son of God.

We froze as the bartender's iPhone flashed, positioned as in *The Last Supper*. They called me Paul, though my name is Derrick. "Paul, Paul, please don't lama sabachthani us." Then they took me to another brick building, filled with apartments outfitted with modern amenities. Wine was passed and pizza sliced. They washed my feet and called me Elohim. Of the twelve, eight were Jews; the remaining four were Lutheran girls, with shoulders for carrying bags of seed, like their ancestors hundreds of years ago when they settled in the frozen land, with thick welcoming hands that could squeeze the milk out of an udder. Their breasts, large and warm, pressed up against my body, all of us on the couch or the floor in the living room. They rubbed my feet as we watched *The Seventh Seal*. Their perfumes smelled of butter and roses. The Lutherans wore knee-high leather boots and tight jeans and sparkly blouses and North Face jackets. The Jews wore clothes from Europe or maybe Cleveland or Detroit or another Rust Belt city, once a powerhouse in manufacturing with repurposed warehouses that have become industrial spaces to construct ripped black jeans or long-brimmed hats.

Around me, they became nude. The Jews did not exclude the Lutherans, and the Lutherans loved the Jews. They disrobed me. They poured oils and fine myrrh over me. Incense started to burn, and we smoked a joint one of the Jews had rolled. The Lutherans partook, as I told them it would not be a sin. I loved their shaved crotches in comparison to the Jews bounty down there. Their underwear and bras and tights sat in piles. We moved to the bedroom that looked out on the city. In the distance across the river a band of moving dots drove along an unseen track. Minneapolis, flittering in the darkness. My disciples took their place, their round asses making indentions against the cool window. It was freezing outside but a sauna in the bedroom from our holy bodies. No lights on, hues of blue hips and white breasts and dark curls. The Lutherans' blonde straight hair.

They writhed as I thought about how I could be the one they'd been looking for. That very day I had been at my lowest point in years, sitting on a bench and waiting, once again the pudgy, balding guy who drank too much and worked at menial hard labor. I thought it would be easy to become a great writer, like owning boxes had been, but the process had made me feel as small as I had ever felt, so I walked in the snow to a bar and ordered an IPA, then another and another, until twelve women walked in, eight Jews and four Lutherans, and sat at a table like the one Michelangelo drew, and invited me in and called me Paul, which is not my name, and took a picture of me and put it on social media, then they brought me to their place for a night of pizza and wine and Netflix and chill as they slowly took off their clothes and kissed each other and washed my feet and rubbed my prick and giggled and chilled and more wine, and smoked that fat joint the Jew rolled, and one of them suggested we all go to the bedroom, where they stood against the window, as in some junior high boy's dream: he tells himself he could never have it in a million years but then he has it, and he tells all his friends who do not believe him. They pushed their glorious interdenominational bottoms against the window, and it was enough to put an end to religious differences, to make every suicide bomber realize there is not something better in the afterlife, this is it. Here and now is all he could ever want. They had tied me to the bed.

"Am I The One?" I asked, and they replied in Aramaic and Hebrew. We had smoked God's grass and learned Gnostic secrets. They all began to walk toward me in unison. I sacrificed my body for them.

The next morning I woke to all kinds of blinding light with an incredible hangover and the recollection of drugs, immense amounts of drugs. My subconscious wanted more than what it was given, then my conscious gained awareness of what had happened. Right in front of my face was snarly hair, dyed too black for white skin. I turned onto my other side and there was a bigger woman whose breath reeked. Encapsulated like in a sleeping bag, I squirmed my way down. There was only one window in the first-floor apartment, not like the wall of windows I'd imagined in my dream, and there was a dingy parking lot. More snow had fallen and I could not remember where I put my clothes. Careful not to wake up the two girthy beauties, I used all my core strength to slither down the bed. Their heft acting as buoys, as if I were a salmon swimming between two lovely bears.

Out on the sidewalk in sleepy St. Paul, my breath was visible. I staggered until my gait became a straight line. Today is the day, I thought as my head spun, to grow balls and join throngs of known novelists and unknown bloggers and unknown novelists and known bloggers and shake hands and say with bright vigor, "Hello, gatekeeper, though you may try and strike me down, I will not abate. I will be back again tomorrow with another manuscript, and this time you will not greet me with the automated lowest-tier response, this time it will be the automated second-tier response, wherein you thank me profusely for submitting and call me by name."

And the day after that I will come back with something else, before the two months I was supposed to wait, and yes that story will also be "not quite the right fit," but I won't stop until every single blogger has gone back to Brooklyn, until I've exhausted every single booth promoting the smallest of journals that no one outside the immediate family and significant other will read. Because once you've met them in person they can pin a face to a name when you query them online, but even if they still don't accept you, well, damn, you tried, you gave it everything you could in pursuit of being a person who writes an essay for a website based in New York City about your journey to become published, and wow, look, now you're out here with everyone else in heaven, the place where the essayist journalist slash novelist blogger short-story writers live.

Walking back to the hotel to shake off last night's toxins, I could not get cynical. That was the old me, and I hated the old me. I walked the streets of the landlocked city, planted on land stolen from the natives, inhabited now by people who should be in Sweden or Norway. They'd be happier there, living under social-ized government, even if they'd change that soon enough. For all their liberal talk, they love money and living the most hygge life-style. As it is known, those who talk about checking their privilege the most are the ones with the most privilege.

It stopped snowing. Light diffused through the haze of the clouds, left over from yesterday's storm, and it was impossibly bright, maybe because of the snow reflecting, or the earth dying, or the abundance of birds in Spain. Who could say. I kept walking as the world spun, uninterested in my pursuit. Still, I was lucky to have what I had and I should not yearn, most would say. But they don't know what happiness is, not for me, as I don't know what happiness is for them. An ant could be happy. Should I be happy to be an ant?

Smell the cold like a pain. Exhaust from a truck. The pant legs of my suit became dirtier, irredeemably so. Buy buy buy. I wanted to purchase the jealousy of others. I don't want more boxes and trim bodies and hundreds of thousands of dollars. I want, when I am fifty and have deteriorated, for artful twentysomethings to trample over each other to be my fling for a week in Paris. Look around and listen to the beat of your heart. Recover, I thought, but not today. Today eat a vegan breakfast in the North Loop and sleep in your sumptuous hotel bed, away from the good-looking plump girls from White Bear Lake. Sleep after chia seeds and cabbage and a kale smoothie, then go and find a box and do what you know better than anyone else at the conference. After that, forward. Watch your step on the icy sidewalks. Don't trip now. Everything is so close. Can you feel it?

I powered through and found a box and after the PR's I took home one of the girls who'd been stretching in the corner on a bouncy ball. But the next morning, on the final day of AWP, I said no more screwing around. I put on a casual outfit, one that said *I am here to learn*, so that I might later come to the conference in a warmer city, Key West or Charleston, and show everyone how foolish they'd been not to see my talents, to so callously not allow me in the group because I was not in the group. I put on 23oz heavy denim jeans, imported from Japan, and my Red Wings and a t-shirt that looked casual and unplanned but accentuated my arms and chest and abs in a way I knew women would notice, and men too, annoyed that some guy would walk around a writing conference with that kind of body. I put on my Canada Goose and my Filson bison-hair stocking hat and left into the quiet hallway, then the mirror-finished steel elevator. A Somali man picked me up and drove me to the same bench and once again I was looking at my phone.

"Screw it," I said out loud. This was after an hour of yearning for more lit-scene followers. The only way to get them was by taking action. Then, as soon as I got in, I wished I was back outside. All the bookish eyes pointed at me, and not in a good way, like at the box when everyone yells for me to set a personal record in dead lift or get that last burpee before the time runs out. A group of college-aged kids laughed in the foyer. Streams of middle-aged women wore long coats and heavy makeup. Bald men clutched worn-out manuscripts. They bumped my shoulders as they crammed by, as if racing to not be forgotten. Way up above, fluorescent lights shined down on rows of desperate tables separated into camps of ideas of what a book is and what it is not, each with fierce ideologies that could start a war in any other culture but here with the feckless wimps and simpering dorks would only cause bickering or at worst a bad book review a few years down the line after the reviewer is sure his career is over and now is free to shit on anything anyone else does.

Meanderingly through the labyrinth, awash in undefined chatter, with the people who, in the best-case scenario, someday when they were long dead, other people would be inspired to go to school and read them, the dead authors. So it goes like that. We're pretending if we say we can teach someone how to write. The best work is created by the autodidacts. Payment or not, they continue. It is their lifeblood, not their livelihood. A sticky film collected on my skin from brushing up against the wretched dreamers. They offered the world their bloated words about addled lives and depraved sexual misadventures and tortured relationships, all of which were brought upon them by themselves. They looked out of shape, slumped off, ashen. The image in my head of the round-assed neophyte just out of her teens bouncing around my bedroom while reading my latest novel about my time in Sudan seemed a myth. Her flawless skin, the product of no creams or lotions, a mirage. Maybe, I thought, I should stick to boxes and keep making money and inwardly rage when I read a limp novel about four Brooklyn guys who love baseball and have gone to Harvard. In my wandering, I came upon a booth the organizers shoved into the corner, one of those small presses with less than five hundred followers on Twitter that want big things, but for whom the greatest achievement will be the nights their unpaid poetry editor reads in front of nine people at an independent coffee shop and afterward a stranger tells them, "Cool poem." At the booth was a huddled mass of Goths in their mid-twenties. They were affected when I approached, as if they had not seen a human in years. One tried to speak but her throat was dry. I offered my water. She took a drink.

"Thank you," she said bleakly. A wind swept through. They were near an exit.

"Can I buy this?" I asked. I picked up every book they sold. "Can I buy them all?" Two of the Goths fainted. The one who'd drunk the water stared at me still.

Later, I dabbed the second Goth's forehead with a tissue as she woke from her daze. I had revived the other. I thought they would stay with their friend, since she was in need and a man loomed in their presence, but they left, and I took the last Goth to her apartment and we made love as a way of mending woes between ruptured sexes. After we were done she walked like a cowboy to the kitchen. But she didn't make it, she came back and got on her knees and begged me to marry her. I told her such declarations of passion could be considered rape culture, and she conceded I was right. She was skinny, with breasts like melons. She asked me to marry her again after she brought us breakfast in bed. I allowed her to pleasure me as many times as she wanted. Once dry, I said farewell to the Cure poster above her bed and Morrissey on the record player and the smell of patchouli in her sad little place.

In a cab with a Somali man, I reviewed what I was. A dead-lift instructor, owner of boxes, self-made, lover of ripped thighs and cord hamstrings, yoga breasts smooshed in Lycra. Once I was fat but I worked my way into the top percentile of those who keep track of their body mass index. In this shape I will live longer, or I won't, as they now say you're as likely to die in a car accident as by gun violence. I bike to my boxes from my high-rise condo in downtown Milwaukee. I live in the Rust Belt so I can afford a cheap place, only nineteen hundred a month, and with that I get a view of Lake Michigan from thirty stories in the air. From up there it looks like an ocean. I travel using the money I earned by pulling myself out of the muck, after working at a steelyard while gaining weight and listlessly floating through life, online dating and drinking. I have been all over this country, and to other countries too, yet I am empty. I long not for God, or a wife, or more money, but adulation. Sycophants. Devotees. I want others to tell me how great I am. I strive to be a novelist. Classify me under "literary fiction."

I checked out of the hotel and said goodbye to Minneapolis and its cold fake veneer. The whole conference filled with fish from the ten thousand lakes who wanted to be in the in, sticking out their fins to see if they could glom on to someone important who talks about writing for a living. Back home in Milwaukee, looking out over a real lake, I poured myself a twenty-six-year-old Scotch and breathed in the frigid air, and peat moss from thousands of miles away lingered in my nostrils. Down with one gulp, like a bog in my mouth or if Band-Aid made a cologne, the warm rushing came. I had returned from a trip where I made love with women and did drugs but did not gain literary contacts. I shouted from my deck, and one of my neighbors shouted back, "Shut it, bitch." The building has retired couples but this was one of the young executives on cocaine. Tomorrow, I thought, I'll start again to seek The One who can show me how to become the kind of person who, if he shouts at a party, no one ever tells him to be quiet. Everyone just sits and marvels at the learned noise.

The next day I took the train to Chicago to meet up with Tatum Spencer, who started life as a boy. God had assigned her wrong, and I understood. I wanted to be muscular and tall and not more than three percent body fat, and to get there I had to work out thirty hours a week for two years, carving myself, like an outdoorsman with a chainsaw and a hunk of wood. But some need to glue on acorns or infuse their bark with sap from a different tree in order to feel whole. Maybe in the future, it won't be that way. Maybe someday we'll choose what we want to be. Or once a religion has taken over the world—inevitable, since those who have the most children are religious and the people who are not barely ever have more than one, and the religious ones teach their children religion, and the not-religious ones teach their one child to think without religion, so one day this earth, if it isn't destroyed by nuclear war, will be hive-minded, but I will be dead, buried and restful, and the ones who cherish art, the few who are left, will visit my grave and lay flowers in the Père Lachaise—that will be impossible, and everyone will have to struggle with whatever parts God gave them. I was in Tatum's neighborhood, Logan Square, and at her front door I rang the buzzer. We had exchanged emails and she'd agreed to answer my questions about what it's like to be a professional sayer of words online.

"The more you talk," she wrote, "the more others assume what you are saying must be correct. We are in an age where the greatest promoters are recognized, not the greatest artists."

"I know, and I know I will never be Nabokov or Joyce or Proust," I wrote to her over email. "My novels will never be called dense. I just need them to be read."

I did not tell Tatum that I wanted others to know about my love of thick thighs and the great pains I have gone through to become an owner of boxes, that there are women I have been with in back rooms who pulled down their shimmering yoga pants and I had them over my desk. In my novel I described their asses, slapping against my pelvis, and the sadness I felt when one left for another box.

I heard someone coming, then tiny footsteps. A pasty woman wearing a cape opened the door. Her face was stained with greasy pimples and she spoke as if she were eating peanut butter. She pointed me down the hallway in the direction of Tatum's office. This was the girlfriend, I assumed. When I got to the office, Tatum did not turn away from her computer. The girlfriend said Tatum would type her answers on the screen.

"She doesn't feel comfortable with maleness," Tatum's girl-friend said.

"I'm sorry," I said, unable to stop looking at the contraption hooked to Tatum's body, a hose going from the computer to her belly.

"It's where she gets her nourishment," the girlfriend said. The room smelled of feminine products, potpourri, and human excrement. I looked at the tube, hooked umbilically into Tatum's belly button. A pink fluid, like a puree, fed into her stomach. The girlfriend could tell I was confused.

"It's a prototype. Tatum is one of the few people in the world to have one. It works by transforming favorites and mentions into food and water. It's what she eats, except for the dog snacks we share with our little noodle."

The malnourished Shih Tzu shuffled in and rested at the feet of the girlfriend, wheezing as it settled down. I thought it might stop breathing if forced to go outside. Tatum stopped typing, and the viscous fluid in her tube slowed. This frightened her girlfriend. She pointed toward the door.

"Tatum doesn't feel safe. You have to leave. You are the patriarchy."

Red buttons were all over the walls. So I carefully left, afraid any act could put me in jail.

The first book I wrote before any fiction was about how to get the most out of your dead lifting by utilizing biofeedback training. My proven method can catapult a man off his floor lifts, jump-starting stagnating numbers. The typical guy who thinks he's doing okay in the mid- to high three hundreds can use my book and shoot himself into the five hundreds and even six hundreds. Dead lifting—lifting a bar from the ground and pulling it to your waist—is the truest test of strength this world has to offer. I've been bedded by strangers after posting videos of my dead-lifting on social media. But all those libidinal encounters were shallow, I know now, and if I am destined to find real love I need to seek women less buff and more well-read, who work their mind not just their body, and maybe they don't call me back the next day because of a capricious mood. But I was weak, so I went to see them anyway.

I drove to the outskirts of Madison, to the closest place to heaven on this earth I have encountered. A commune of thick glutes and fibrous hamstrings and hair in ponytails and braids, and after one last time, I bargained with myself, my more continental tastes would flourish: I would stay up late, start smoking, and fail to get the recommended ten hours of sleep. Eat whatever I please. I happened across this hedonistic commune a few years ago when I was starting to buy boxes in the region. I had passed through Madison to meet with a realtor, and she referred me to a yoga studio. The head yogi couldn't have been more than twenty-two, and she showed me the way to her house by taking dirt roads. Once there, I was inundated with free-flowing aesthetes saluting the sky, then coming inside to rub on each other, then going back out in the garden to pull vegetables. They ambulated and made stews and smoked weed and went to their rooms at night to be with a man who had happened upon that farm as mystical as Oz.

When I got there this time, the woman at the front door did not wear a sarong, and her breasts were covered, if by a chiffon blouse. Things had changed. They now had an official sign touting "Massage and Organic Foods." They were a company. Hedonism bought and sold. Which was fine, I thought, as I drove back to Milwaukee: everyone needs to grow up. I should too. Find a wife with whom I argue with about schedules and dinner and ogling other forms. I had gone to the farm in Dane County in the hopes someone from the yarn of yogis, as I think that's what you call a group of them, would be there, still stuck at the age of twenty, fit from daily manual labor and tan from the gentle sun, but flexible and soft from the hours of limbering stretches, emanating inner peace from the meditation and weed that grew under a canopy in the shelterbelt. Jealousy did not mar their relationships. Love went from one to the next and no one owned anything or could put a stamp on anyone. I remember I once went to bed with one at night and in the morning found another sweet maiden had slipped between the warm sheets, and that was not only accepted but celebrated, and discussed at the wooden breakfast table with those who had managed to find their way to paradise, telling of the previous night's carnalities—knowing the sound of a certain climax through the paper-thin walls—while eating fresh jams and homemade breads and bacon from the pigs oinking in the barn. I would have lived there, but only women were allowed, even if some men visited frequently enough that they may as well have.

What's my problem, I thought on drive back on I-94, with insane Wisconsin drivers whizzing past me. Why can't I give up on my dream of becoming a novelist and be happy with what I have? I could teach classes at the box, expounding on the nuances between push presses and push jerks and cleans and power cleans, telling my young students about the calluses on my palms from pulls on the rig. But what I would like to do, instead of being jacked and having women want me for my body and money, is to have them want me for my insights about the world, and after that to gain status from the sale of my literary fiction. Now, with all my physical power, I am apt to think I am a superman. Years ago, before becoming what I am today, I saw life as Jean Rhys did: "I'd planned to die at thirty... and then you go on and on and on. It's difficult. Too much trouble."

There was a time when I didn't want to live, when I was fat and unaccomplished, and now almost ten years later I have everything I could ever want, and yet I want more. I should live my life like in a modern novel where I become a prostitute and am devoid of human emotion. And why can't I? Do I need more heroin? As a teen I should have had richer parents who let me take any substance, so that now I'd be disconnected and live in a bland flatness where nothing affects me. That'd be the best for me. I wouldn't have all these dreams of trying to make it. I wouldn't want to now stop my Audi and walk away from the interstate and into a field and sit down in the snow, thinking of the failure of my first self-published novel.

I got back to Milwaukee in the middle of December and thought of going on a long run. Really what I should have been doing was starting on my next novel of semi-autobiographical fiction. My first is about a guy who owns boxes and has dalliances with fit women. One of them gets upset when she finds the head instructor with someone else in the back room; she sees only the shaved ass of the instructor, and the legs of the other girl with her yoga pants around her ankles, and this other girl's yelps are so theatrical it's like she is getting rammed with an oil drill.

Fitzgerald said every writer has two or three stories to tell, and they're lucky they get to tell them over and over. What could be my other two, or even three? I could write about my upbringing, how I got to be this and not that. I called Mary instead.

"No later than nine," Mary said, so I took my time in the shower, and as the hot water rolled over me all aspiration evaporated, knowing who was coming and how well she treated me.

Dried and powdered, sitting in my Eames chair from the Herman Miller Collection next to the floor-to-ceiling windows, I admired the lake. Even after the conference and the trip to Chicago and Madison and other places I have not mentioned, like Iowa City and New York and Oxford, I still did not have anyone to whom I could personally address my submission to *Granta*. I'd made love to MFA candidates who didn't know a thing other than ass-fucking. They said that was "the most literate way to make love." A falcon landed on the flower pot on my balcony as I worried that the sex had not been good enough for them, and the bird flew away. Mary, the newspaper reporter, would lighten my spirits.

She worked out at one of my boxes. Fifteen pounds overweight, Mary never had the energy to come to class regularly or give full effort, and I loved that. She was airheaded after all the weed she smoked. She showed up smelling like perfume and sex, and we ordered pizza and smoked and made out for a while. When the pizza arrived we ate and talked about a blog she wrote for, based in Minneapolis. She accused its editors of being elitist. I listened for what seemed like days As the drugs had kicked in, my abs distended, my belly content. I looked at the dark lake, the city, and I used the remote to turn the recessed lights down low. She continued about how on their About page they said they loved hanging out with their writers but when she reached out to meet for drinks, no one responded, and they didn't even follow her on social media, even after she'd written seven posts, with one of them getting the most likes of all their recent posts.

"And the final straw is when I submitted my post about dom-sub stuff, Jay said it wasn't 'what they were looking for.' I think it emotionally scarred him."

She giggled and took another bite of pizza and I began to imagine what kind of underwear she had worn. She always wore underwear that someone who was lucky got to see. For some reason she saved them for our nights, or maybe she spent a lot of her income on fragile undergarments and weed. She did not own a car. She ate constantly and biked everywhere, and I think that's how she stayed thick and delicious, with stumps for legs and hams for glutes and nubs for breasts, with a pooch from too many nights like the ones we were having. She hated CrossFit. Still, I loved touching her, the way the softness enveloped and the strength beneath spurred me on.

We played video games—I own everything she wants to play—on a screen five times bigger than the microwave-sized one in her shared house in Riverwest. I was touching the inside of her thigh, pushing up her tweed skirt. She bit her lip as she began to pay less attention to the stolen car on the screen, letting out a moan as her character stopped moving. She began doing a thing she does, where she licks her lips and zones out by not playing the game for a few seconds. I kneeled and pulled down her tights and found she had worn a white pair with red hearts, and before pulling them down I breathed on her while she flexed her leg muscles and rubbed my hair. She let out an "ohhh," as if already near the end. So sweet. Not long after that I was slamming my prick into her throat, making her choke while slapping her face, her curls pulled back. I did not come, and carried her over to the window where I pushed her hips up and I don't know how long we were there. Her legs wobbled, as if she could not take anymore, and so I flipped her around and finished on her face. She kept my love on her as we went to my balcony, some falling to the sidewalk below. We stood there for a few minutes, and I held her warm body from behind, the cold breeze going over us. The sky was black, and I wondered, as I could not stop wondering, who those blog people were, and whether Mary could give me their information.

For a long time I was optimistic. For almost ten years everything went right. I went back to school and received my MBA. My first box took off, and I bought another. I became wealthy and got in shape. Having a woman became as easy as taking a breath. Then, about six months ago, I self-published a novel and started on this search to find The One in charge of who gets noticed and who doesn't in the world of blogs and opinions and thoughts, how some get vaunted and praised and others are forgotten. I should have listened to Mary, but I didn't. Even after the conference, I thought they would like me. In grade school everyone likes each other, all of us going to the same sleepovers. Everyone gets a Valentine, as long as they don't smell. In my twenties I thought, as long as I was myself, it would be the same, and the few who didn't like me would be the jerks. As I march through my late thirties, very close to forty, I have found not as many like you just because you're you.

After leaving the disaffected bloggers with their free food and drinks, I went to my car and sat in the Minneapolis winter. I stayed there for hours, until the whole city was quiet. No more packs of huddled coat-wearing millennials breathing out smoke in puffs, the cold muting their voices. They'd gone home to drink whiskey and cuddle up and touch each other until they woke up in the morning and went to brunch. If you'd asked me a few months ago to find The One in charge of the writing world, I would have taken to that task like a starving mountain lion chasing after an elk, just like I did with my body years ago, turning it from a sack of blubber into a piece of marble. Just like I did with my money, starting with almost nothing and turning it into the fat bank statement it is today, going from a guy who always texted first and never heard anything back to a guy who never texts first and always hears back.

In my freezing Audi, I found myself not caring, and I thought, Whoever he or she is who is in charge of becoming known and not unknown, I should leave them be. That person is sad and poor, and if they do make any money they are beholden to a media conglomerate to project the opinion of the powers-that-be in order to create an illusion so as to attract readers of a certain worldview to said conglomerate. And if they write books, that's worse. One does not write words unprovoked, if at peace. There is no need for such endless hand-wringing. And if you're a genre writer, you don't get critical acclaim, so what's the point? Easier professions must exist than ghostwriting romance. The mental strain of knowing every day one has to sit down and create situations and emotions and actions from nothing must be exhausting. Why not sell stocks or trade land? As for the "writer's writers," they teach. Think of how miserable those people are and yet how happy they pretend to be, and there I was straining to be one of them, reaching out to the heavens to answer my prayer to be in the in and not on the outs.

I started my Audi and drove on the barren interstate at three in the morning, and as I crossed the St. Croix my next novel appeared to me. I had written about splaying women who worked out at my boxes, jumping them up on the chin-up bar and having them hang there for as long as they could while I ate their asses. I thought of what else I could say as I free-associated in my purring vehicle. The darkened Chippewa Valley around me, here is what came to me:

> Everything can mean everything and nothing can mean frogs and I like turtles so let's all go to the fair for thousands of frankels until we reach the part where someone in a tweed coat gives us half a million to repump our pumping parts. If this isn't making any sense yet that's okay we've just started and you have so much time to get so much more confried and smear cheese curds on our faces with me in Wisconsin where we'll travel up to the north words and commune with the gerund wolves who spit up their hunts of participle squirrels.

It was the start of something great, I just knew it. And I drove home happy.

Chloe worked as a blogger for *Teen Vogue* but used to write for a website that Paul, the author of this story out there peeking in like a pervert, once wrote for, a confessional blogging platform a gay man in New York City started by sending links to his mushroom-taking friends, who spread it to their friends across the country, until it turned into a list factory geared toward high school girls about how the struggle was real and relationships were hard. Chloe wrote five articles for the website and skyrocketed in popularity and was hired on full-time in the span of a week, while Paul, the flesh sack typing my thoughts, wrote articles and personal essays and lists for almost two years. For free he did that, never getting farther than excited if they publicized one of his hundreds of posts on social media. After three years, he finally petered out and faded into obscurity, with producers from the site unfollowing him until it was like no one had ever known him at all.

I was lucky to be traveling to see Chloe, a winner, unlike Paul. I own boxes, and live stories up in the sky. I bed women with bubble butts. I can do a hundred consecutive triple-unders, and I could do more. My dong is too big for some women, they have said, and I have money to travel at will. There is no reason I should be timid around Chloe. She is a girl wandering around, walking into rooms and saying things, sitting down and typing words. Now Paul wants to describe me going to Ella's apartment in New York City now, and how, when I show up, we start having sex. It's the kind of magical nonsense he always railed against, the lazy absurdism that is a mixture of the natural world with a wild world where, "you know, it's fiction, so anything can happen," but he is unable to create scenes to form a narrative that paints a picture of seamless imagination that could be witnessed in real life but hasn't occurred—or has, in alternate composite ways—because it is fiction. Doing that takes time and hard work. And Paul once had the will to attempt to conjure up such a story, but now he is so beaten down and fat and old and unknown that all he can manage is a CrossFit guy who goes around having sex with all the women Paul himself wants. Paul wants to know what it's like to have six-pack abs and a cock like a road and so much money he doesn't know what to do with it. Also, if I could speculate, he wants to make fun of other writers, because he doesn't like any other writers. I can read his mind and feel the weight of his head resting against the keys of the keyboard, his face red and sweaty, pushing keys in utter exasperation because he has tried for years but the man is full of typos and now a loser who was once in constant limerence while online dating, losing out on attractive young ladies who were crushed by the weight of his smothering instant affection. I am the one who owns boxes and is ripped and travels to New York to see bloggers. He is trying to hemorrhage a scene out of his brain, malformed and squishy and unappealing.

Chloe opened the door, and before I could even ask a question her lips were around my prick. She slobbered, making a noise like a hose losing and gaining pressure. Periodically I took a break from looking down at her to scan her pristine apartment. The brick walls, the supporting brick beams, the MacBook on the coffee table, a bookshelf with classics and modern bores that stupefied most guys. Chloe had long straight black hair, perpetually brown skin, and a shape like an hourglass. We finished in her bedroom, where the walls were hung with abstract art her friends made in college and a movie poster for *Beaches*. She had a jewelry box and a bed with a downy white comforter, a view of a park and restaurants and bars.

"I don't normally fuck guys who tell me how great a writer I am." She was lying. We all do. Chloe was pretty, but not so far above human indignity that she would always be able to resist guys who came across one of her posts about dating and complimented her.

"I don't normally do this either," I said. Now everyone had lied. "I came here to see you, but also I was wondering if you knew the person in charge of book deals. Or maybe that's not how to say it. I want The One?"

"Like the Matrix?" Her breasts were pristine and motionless. But I liked them better before, when I had her on all fours and they swung in unpredictable figure eights.

"Well, sort of. I mean to ask, how does one get famous as a writer? Who's in charge of who gets known? It seems random, doesn't it?"

But Chloe had started sucking on me again, and when I'd finished a second time I put on my clothes as quickly as I could and left---knowing she would only start again soon---the remaining seed from my prick dangling like a stubborn hair.

Paul has been scouring the internet for pictures of women who look real for a while now. He started at the website he drooled over back in 2011, the one where they all look like someone he might have seen on OkCupid: tattooed, posing in their apartments wearing their best underwear, with tan lines and bushes and breasts, big and swinging or flat and athletic, but always with hefty rear ends, the kind Paul wanted to bite into as he clicked around but instead he bit his own tongue out of fright, knowing these creatures wandered the earth and he would never know or talk to them or smell between their cheeks of their ass. It started on that website with a model named Ross Carey, a bit older than the rest, approaching thirty or just on the other side of it, with bountiful pubic hair, and see-through eggshell-blue panties, and tan lines, and goose bumps on the insides of her upper thighs.

"Must have been cold," Paul reasoned.

Paul, I know, plans on taking his phone to the bathroom to finish. Then I'll be stuck here, with nothing to do. Strange, how I invade Paul's world. I embarked on this voyage to see if I could uncover the reason why he is a pathetic failure by scratching at why some are published and others are unknown. Long ago, he started writing because he wanted to describe the time he fell in love with The One sent by God, but she told him to pray for another, and now it's just him daydreaming in his apartment many years later, alone, lusting over strangers' asses. This woman he sees is not the most attractive of the women who pose mostly nude for this website which caters to men like Paul who do not want to masturbate to unreal ideations. She has kept her pubic hair, and she has a wide curving mouth and a healthy Angus beef to her hindquarters. The tan lines make the whole prospect of grabbing her behind more exciting, I'm sure; even I'd want someone with more definition in her arms and glutes, and not such dowdy hair, parted down the middle. She looks like someone who is careful with what she eats and does the occasional yoga class, but not religiously. Me, I'd prefer an ass suspended in their air like a puppet lifted by invisible strings. This one is more homey and is attached to a woman who teaches other women how to orgasm. Still, it's easy to see, she is someone with whom to cuddle after a ten-year-anniversary dinner. That's the kind of thing Paul seems obsessed with, to have that. I see him staring at this computer, thinking of what to write after a day at his office job where he enters data, racked with anxiety and guilt over things that didn't happen. I think he wants to write a significant paragraph, even a word, but he can't. The best he can do is Google Ross Carey and stave off the urge to masturbate, envisioning his spurts flying onto her smiling visage, dotting and lining her lips and cheeks.

"What am I doing here?" I asked the door of the home of a woman I'd happened across online. Her website said she held conventions in her apartment where she taught women how to orgasm. My business is getting people into shape physically, so why not have a gym to get into shape sexually?

Her name was Ross and she'd asked me to her place after I liked one of her pictures on Instagram, emailing me to say she wanted to choke on me while her husband watched. So I bought a plane ticket to Portland and found myself at her door. Ringing the doorbell wouldn't bring me closer to the person in charge of who gets noticed as a writer, but a detour along the way couldn't hurt, I thought, and I'd never cuckolded.

"Hi," the husband greeted me. He was a beta with a long beard, and couldn't have weighed more than 150 pounds. There was the smell of baby powder on him.

"Hi," I replied. "Ready to watch me fuck?" And I thrust my hips and moved my arms like I was skiing with poles. Too brash, I knew it, but I wanted to break the ice. The husband timidly grimaced and politely showed me into the house, offered me tea and told me his wife would be ready soon. I could hear the shower running. We sat down at a wooden table, nothing on it except for a vase with yellow daisies. We talked about the weather.

"Didn't know you guys got snow in Portland."

"We don't, normally," the husband said. "But global warming affects everything."

"I see. Well, the flowers are nice," I was switching the subject, and he appreciated that, I think. He went on about how he got them at their farmers market, how they'd love to go back with me in the morning.

"For sure," I said, even if I knew I would be gone.

The shower turned off and there was the sound of a blow-dryer. Snowflakes fell outside their kitchen window. Lit candles smelled vaguely like cinnamon, the smell of perfume now wafting in. The husband was talking about water rights in the Congo as she padded into the room, and though I hadn't totally understood before why I had come to Portland, it made sense when I saw her. She wore see-through underwear, with no bra, her arms covering her breasts. A vision.

"Are you ready to fuck my brains out?" she asked. The husband was taking off his pants, the clicking of his belt against the metal of his zipper. She looked at him, then at me. "I hope you feel the same."

In the late morning I slunk out of the bedroom, passing the husband immobilized with his wrists tied behind a radiator so all he could do was protest. At some point, I hoped, he would be allowed to relieve himself. If I had a wife as grown as Ross, who did the things she did, jealousy would eat at me so strongly I'd become the Hulk and snap out of my constraints, chase away the other man, maybe even strangle him with the bed sheet, making my wife so enraged with feral hormones that all she could do was get on all fours and pant, and with just one thrust send her into oblivion. But I'm not him, and I don't know what it's like to live with a woman who teaches orgasm classes, having to hear about them until they become as routine as taking out the trash.

Before I left, a strange thing did happen. At some somnolent moment around dawn, after my prick's last sputtering like a dying engine, she wiped everything off with her hand and licked each of her fingers like eating barbeque and went right back to sleep. I could look to the foot of the bed and see the husband slumped over, like a sack of potatoes on the floor. The strange thing happened minutes later, on the last time in the early morning when she intimately slid on top of me like in a dream, her face all close. The other times had been animalistic, hardly ever kissing each other except for the interment attention to our private areas. This time she whispered in my ear as she rode, her warm torso and thighs, "You're looking in the wrong place."

I worried she was speaking of my abilities, that I was not touching her in the right quadrant to engage a specific euphoria, as she'd learned from her teacher and guru, a feminist icon from the '70s. That couldn't have been it, though, by the way she looked at me and transferred everything.

"Don't look around," she said without speaking. "Look inward." Then she did say out loud, "Eat my cunt."

So I did, and she tasted like mango, and took my last triumph inside her. Then I fell asleep. Exhausted, I went into dreaming with the mantra: *Look inward. Be free of thoughts. Be free.*

At the Portland airport I bought a ticket to Bora-Bora, to meditate on what Ross had told me. Once there, I moved into a thatch-roofed cabana jutting out into the ocean. The green-blue waters surrounding me, I ate my breakfast of fresh fruit and scrambled eggs with bloody marys infused with divine spices, brought to me by canoe by gorgeous islanders in grass skirts. I took a swim in the undisturbed warm waters, then back up for another tropical drink, a nap and a sunbath in the nude, attracting wives on their honeymoons, then another swim, then another drink, followed by a late-night party with the wives, interspersed with the brown islanders who worked at the resort, all of us sun-tinged and spilling our love out into the endless miles of ocean, where only the whales and dolphins heard and tasted.

Days of that, I began to sense a figure watching from one of the other huts. As a man now versed in cuckolding, I at first thought one of the husbands was spying on us, jealous that his trim new bride had come into my hut wearing her twinkling diamond ring. But as we continued to drive deeper into one another and they kissed young breasts and licked each other's asses, I sensed it was not a husband at all, that the one who watched us was a ghost. I took a breather from the bacchanalia and looked out at my personal pier that also served also as my diving board, and saw a face, shrouded by the darkness, on the other side of the circle of paradise buffered by translucent waters. Another gorgeous woman appeared and distracted me. She dove into the water without a splash and swam over and joined our revelry. All the girls greeted her with laughter and groping. She had the largest breasts and the biggest bush. We all gawked.

In the morning and surrounded by bodies strewn about the room like unfolded laundry, I got up and took a swim. Floating on my back I looked up at the heavens, stars in them still, and wondered why anyone strived for anything at all. We should all be so lucky to experience anything, like the newlywed brides I deflowered the night before, the crystalline waters buoying me, and the light streaming from a million years away. All those events happening together at once, and I was a molecule among them. The brides had come over in boy shorts and thongs. They said they had seen me and found themselves coveting what I could give, the single life they lived before they anchored themselves to one man. The sun was coming up, and I swam out to the ocean as though pulled by a magnet. I grabbed onto a wooden pile, but it was no use. I was catapulted out into the sea. An ominous presence took hold of the placid beauty, and I knew the ghost in the other hut had been Paul, who engineered my drowning. I was calm, even as I swallowed the water. I know he thinks this story will save him and one day be read by other sad cases wanting to be with twenty-two-year-olds who pose for blogs featuring their apartments, who listen to records and do yoga and majored in French and might apply for their MFA in dance. He has to keep me alive for at least a hundred thousand words, even if we all know he might not even make it half that far. A giant wave picked me up and pushed me close enough to the resort. I swam the rest of the way.

Weeks passed, and the newlyweds went home. I packed up my things, read the angry notes left by the husbands. I scrolled through the secret numbers and accompanying pictures in my phone. The picture I loved the most? A group one where they all covered parts of themselves in the cool shade of my bedroom, the sun inching in and making a triangle on the floor. A fake shocked expression on each but my favorite was laughing, her arms at her side, every inch of her exposed. Soon enough, I was back home in Milwaukee, never to see her again.

I had sex with two from one of my boxes in the hopes of getting over the heartbreak of leaving my love in Bora-Bora. It didn't work, but I tried. They came over—I texted from the plane—with bottles of wine from Whole Foods to warm our cold bones in the city by the lake. They showed me everything my box had taught them: handstand walks in yoga pants, burpees with no underwear, slapping their asses up and down on my prick, twice in a row like a double-under. In the morning they slept by each other, their muscular bodies a shining example, and I went out to my balcony to smoke more of the weed they'd brought. In my terrycloth robe I took in the hazy waters, deep blues that were almost black, and knew that at any second Paul could send an axe to fall out of the sky and onto my head.

I stood and enjoyed the high, and afterward went inside to write my next novel that will at least be more successful than this drivel. My favorite writers are Bob Lue, Gloria Emily, and Ayn Rand. I am a Republican who loves drugs and smashing pussy and Gloria and Ayn and Bob would agree those things are great. They are not concerned with prose, the kind a soaking novelist writes on a damp sheet of paper with a dull crayon. And so I began to create art that embodied their spirits, and even if I fell short of capturing their essences, just droplets of their spit would be better than what Paul could get if we multiplied him by a million. To openly insult him is strange, as if I am gaining sway, and in the next moment I found myself back in the bedroom being pegged by the two strong CrossFit women, their thrusts as vigorous as any man's. They took turns wearing the belt and plugging my ass, and I must have told them I wanted it, because they were saying, "That's how you want it, you dirty little whore," and I could not tell them otherwise.

After that morning of being rammed mercilessly and gaining an appreciation for the art, I had the urge to travel, to shake hands with someone who might want to sell my homage to the greatness of Ayn Rand and Bob Lue and Gloria Emily. I finished the novel that afternoon on a memory foam seat cushion in a great whirlwind of inspiration. The papers, all printed out, made a neat stack on my oak dining-room table. I took a picture and posted it to my writer Instagram. It received only a portion of the likes a post from the beach in Bora-Bora got on my fitness Instagram, but I could suffer for now. The next day I traveled to the greatest city. Not in the South, where they love the smell of their farts, and or the Midwest, with those writers who are rapturous about flat ground and required to complain about how other people consider where they live "flyover country." And you don't want to be one of those West Coast post-apocalyptics, telling us how Hollywood-porn-stars-turned-reality-TV-stars are bringing about the end of the world. Be a New York City writer, and have an ancestor who came over on the *Mayflower or suffered in the Holocaust.*

How glorious it was, going into a building with a zip code with 1's and 0's. Through the revolving doors, I did not show identification to anyone. The security person nodded and I headed straight to the elevator. A woman hopped on, and before the doors closed she began to unbutton her white blouse to reveal a red bra. She wore a wool skirt and flipped it up, then pushed down her tiny red underwear. She bent over, her supple ass pushing against me. She was tanned, or had gone on a trip somewhere warm, with a tantalizing outline where a bikini would have been. I was afraid of the doors opening but they stayed interminably closed, as if we were going up forever, as if time did not exist, and she reached around and took out my cock. A minute went by before she wailed, and right as she stood up the doors opened, and she walked out into the marketing arm of a publishing house, buttoning her blouse. She could not have been more than twenty-one, perhaps an intern taking her winter break from college. She attended Vassar, not Wellesley. She was too attractive. I went further up, hoping for no more stops, but right as I hoped for that the elevator stopped and a woman who looked like she was in charge of a division dropped down on her knees, taking off her blazer and black shirt, revealing her torpedoes. She jacked me off and I came on her chest. She put her shirt back on and her blazer too. On the next floor a man and a woman, two copyright lawyers, I think, got on and started making out against the chrome walls. The woman grabbed my prick and said she ached but I hardly had enough rigidity left to give more than a couple weak pumps, and the man felt sorry for me, I could tell. When he left the elevator he was whispering to the woman.

I jumped out behind them to find the stairs and ran up to the floor with the agents, even if, as I have been told by the editor who looked over my self-published novel, agents and publishers don't normally share the same building. As soon as I walked in, every woman in the office jumped up, sniffing at the air like wolves hunting. I froze. They did not just want my novel about the Crossfitters I have bedded. They wanted me. I ran back down the stairs at full speed.

Paul, I know, made it impossible for me to walk unmolested throughout the offices. He is the one who concocted the slinky-haired, milky-skinned, flesh-desiring archetypes, who might be, on a good day, one in a thousand, but on that day in that skyscraper they came ravenously in a pack, licking their lips and frothing at the mouth, chasing after me like murderers, so I had to sprint down the stairway. How I made it back, I don't know. I only know I am now home in Milwaukee in the nude, looking at a bank statement on my phone from my balcony overlooking the lake, appreciating the swell of numbers, the increasing commas and the freedom they give. At the same time I am aware, through some sentience half-formed in an ether of space and time that goes unseen, of what Paul did for his weekend.

It had been a dream of his since puberty to hear a stranger's noises, but he never did, not in college as a virgin, or after, while working at a Christian group home in Nebraska, or after that, when he moved to Sioux Falls and lived in a studio apartment, or after that, still in Sioux Falls, when he lived in a duplex off Phillips Avenue in McKennan Park where on the bottom level lived a couple---a goateed man and a plump woman---and he never heard a peep waft up through the vents, and he would have listened well, since by then Paul had relinquished his faith in Christ and the commandments given in the New Testament, that if one lusts in their heart they have sinned, and hearing the moans of a full-grown woman would have been breaking a law. Or after that, when he moved to Seattle, into a house with liberals who attended a post-religious Episcopal church, heavy on ceremony and light on theology. One of them entertained a orange-haired young man who played the bongos. He stayed over on Friday nights normally, but all Paul ever heard was when they woke up on Saturday, the cloying sound of laughter after the bongo player tickled the blonde woman, whose outfit always consisted of a sarong, plain white top, dashiki, and bandana. She was attractive, Paul thought, and he would have liked to hear what she sounded like in rapture. But he never did. The other women lived in hermetic solitude, studying the Bible or tarot cards, both of which they believed when it suited them. Or after that, when he moved away from that commune to a basement in Beacon Hill that he found on Craigslist. A lesbian lived upstairs, but she never had women over in the time Paul lived there. He only ever heard her stomping her feet from the kitchen to her bedroom, where she played *World of Warcraft* as a job, it seemed. Or after that, when he moved to Minneapolis suburb of Richfield, into a house with two other men, one on the main floor and the other in the basement, with Paul in the attic. Not once did he catch a murmur of sex, just the tapping of keyboards from the two men preparing themselves for a move to Silicon Valley where they eventually sold the promise of their app to venture capitalists and have since become wealthy and by now must have women over to their smart homes and through mechanical manipulation summon breathy coos, like air from a bellows up the flue, followed by the wails. Or after that, when Paul moved from the suburbs to the Nordeast Minneapolis, where he assumed he would have to put up with the occasional yelp from downstairs while living above two women, girls really, just out of college. Together they hardly weighed more than two hundred pounds, one white and one Asian, and both "cute as a button," as the realtor who showed Paul the place said, but never, not in the year and a half Paul lived there, did he ever hear either of them come close. He only put up with the sounds of their dog, who when they let it out in the front yard barked relentlessly and made brown stains in the grass like crop circles. Paul knew men sifted through the house, their trucks or cars parked on the street, but he never heard a peep. The paucity of sound made Paul think the youth of today were becoming meek and mild, or choosing to simply cut to the chase and give only head to the men.

Only after two years of living with his wife in Milwaukee, where he now lives across the street from me, did he finally hear the noises. In the middle of the night, just past three in the morning, Paul woke to his wife looking at him in the dark. From above, where all they ever heard was the clip-clopping of their neighbor's high heels early in the morning, there was the slow organic building of heavy breathing: enraptured vowels, a half-assembled yes. Paul's wife and he had talked at length about how he never heard a stranger but always wanted to, while his wife did hear the noises at various apartments in Chicago through the years. She said, "Listen, she's banging up there," and Paul was so excited he did not breathe. Just as soon, it stopped. A few minutes later the sounds started again, and again Paul held his breath, and they increased and for a second Paul thought he might hear the end, but again the noises ebbed, and did not return. For a while afterward husband and wife lay in bed, pretending to sleep, but both of them were preoccupied by the sounds of the probably, by all indicators—the heels, where she lived, how she sounded—attractive young woman at the height of her powers. Her calls were hints for anyone within ear's reach, if they had red blood flowing through them, and so Paul took his hand and put it over his wife's bedtime pajamas, and she rolled over and took hold of his hard prick, since he wore no clothes to bed.

I can see him beyond his screen wishing, imploring himself to come up with some kind of scene for me, anything other than thinking the sounds, or sex with a yoga instructor with strong gams and a butt like two yams—why so much rhyming, he thinks—but he can't. I see him there, fawning over a Belgian, a self-proclaimed "Frenchie" who "loves her ass." He is biting his knuckles over her, her hair curling down her neck and shoulders. She is maybe twenty, with the backside of a squats instructor who has an obsession with lingerie.

"She is just out there in the world somewhere," Paul laments.

He wants to give her a chalet and watch as she practices yoga in the nude, sunbathes on a beach along the Côte d'Azur while the Euros in their Speedos bite their knuckles, but no amount of promises could ever sway her, because she is in love with Paul, and just Paul. All these ridiculous things he is thinking instead of creating the next action for me. So I am dangling, as if in an absurd video game, spinning like a pinwheel, haphazardly running into things and falling out in the abyss and into the lake, without any hope of finding the one in charge of who gets noticed and who doesn't.

I woke up in bed with Haylie the Belgian, an underwear model slash fitness junkie of twenty years, her curly hair falling past her shoulders, with a bulbous ass and an impossibly thin tan line circling her waist, a tiny triangle starting just above her coccyx, the rest of her all brown, demarcating her from my white bed sheets and comforter. The snow, and the cold wind. She slept soundly. I must have put her into a deep coma.

I can tell still Paul wants to know if he can, by process of fictionalizing, find the source of all power when it comes to who makes it possible for some to be known and others to flounder, and maybe even beyond, to see if he can locate within the universe what it means to work for something and what it means to just let it happen. If some people are born with a bad set of circumstances that will always block them from their ultimate goal, or, in Paul's case, if the problem originates from the fact that he doesn't write the kind of fiction women want to read, and women are the ones who buy fiction, so he is never going to be successful. He cannot create characters who like riding trains and have taken up a new career in bird-watching in a story that involves switching a sample of birds with another, causing a mix-up that is not unraveled until the very end, at which point it is also revealed that the main character has been in love with the main butterfly catcher the whole time but didn't want to admit that to herself. If he could write a story like that he would have made it, but he can't. He can only write autobiographical sex scenes, and there is not enough to mine for even a full novel.

Out of curiosity I followed Paul today, and I know what you're thinking. Why didn't I just stay in my California King Bed by Autoban under my Downright Eliasa duvet with Grade A Icelandic eiderdown that is guaranteed hypoallergenic, its 434-thread-count silk exterior with flowering vine pattern, so sweet, and the Egyptian cotton sheets and my four Downright Eliasa Canadian White Goose Down King firm and full pillows, contrasting against my firm tan limbs and torso with all the colorful tattoos swirling up my legs and arms and pointing down toward my crotch all waxed and not prickly, watching the money from my boxes pile up in my bank account while Haylie and I smoke weed and gorge ourselves on each other and smoke more weed and eat delivery pizza and pho and waffles? But I have done that a million times, and while Haylie is heaven-sent, and the way her ass is shaped does make my eyes water, I need to be able to see. It can get old being blinded by my ducts reacting to her vibrating ass. That might seem ridiculous, but not if you're me.

I saw Paul get up from the couch in the morning after rehashing an old argument with his wife about texting with an ex-girlfriend. From there he went through the bedroom to the bathroom for a shower. After that, he dressed, then left for work without a sound. He went out into the cold, the winds from the freezing lake drifting over the water like steam. The sun brilliant, blinding from the snow, as the half-drunk cheese-infused citizens bustled to their cars to get to jobs so they might be able to buy their families more cheese. Paul walked to his vehicle blocks away, his face pinching from the elements. He wiped off the snow on the windshield and sat inside while the engine warmed, switching between blubbering sports talk radio and far-right Christian talk radio. He drove to work, the building situated in a poor western suburb, and ran into Walmart for breakfast burritos, and Hot Tamales to cover the taste of the burritos. He bought a can of Coke from the machine and walked upstairs, carrying his foodstuffs in the hopes he could go home early.

Walking between the rows of cubicles, he said good morning and received mumbled hellos in return. He sat down in his gray cubicle, decorated with three magnets from countries in the Caribbean given to him by coworkers who had gone on vacation. He pulled out a stack of files, and I was starting to fall asleep. Even if I could have stayed awake enough to relay his thoughts as he went through the manila folders and client information, periodically answering the phone, they would not be worth recording. And they would have to be pretty damn interesting to trump the terrifying monotony on display in the office, where the main topic was how the other workers went to surrounding small towns to buy tickets for the lottery. That conversation took up the whole day, until Paul left at around two in the afternoon, having spent the last hour fruitlessly checking his email. It frustrated him so much that he deleted all of his emails in a mad purge. That moment was the most exciting part not just of his day, but of his year.

At two o'clock he drove home over salt-covered roads and parked blocks away from his apartment building, which was only three stories high, and walked inside the red brick building and undressed and pooped and afterward searched for "yoga sex," then masturbated to a woman with dreads and a redhead with two black men beside a pool, both with larger members than the one Paul handled. Afterward Paul lay there on the bed, feeling the best he'd felt all day. He got up and showered and dressed in shorts and went to the kitchen and devoured one cold brat, then put three more on the stovetop grill while he watched Premier League football. When the brats finished cooking he put them in three separate pretzel buns and ate them and washed down the taste with a lime-green soda while he watched more soccer. Then he brewed tea and finally sat down at his Martha Stewart Collection desk from Staples and started to aimlessly search through Twitter, rage spewing out of his ears when he came across people much younger who worked as writers. He typed drafts of tweets mocking them but never posted them.

At that point I shut it off—my ability to watch him works like television—and I went back to Haylie. We went for hours, then she vanished to Brussels so as to not make her legion of adoring teenaged boys wait online any longer as they touched themselves in anticipation of her voluptuous form. Paul had gone to one of the boxes I own. He stretched using a PVC pipe in a circle with about ten fit women and one guy more overweight than Paul. The women all in spandex, but with no one there to show off to I heard them think, "Why did I bother wearing my best tights when I could have worn comfortable sweatpants and a baggy t-shirt and it would have been just as well?"

I watched the overweight author stretch. His bones cracked, and I heard him groaning as he put down the PVC pipe and elongated his back to loosen up his thoracic. I caught him trying to take in the ass of the woman stretching next to him. She had a mannish face and a breathtaking body and wore purple tights. I watched later as the girls paired off and lifted while Paul and the other flabby man lifted on their own. There was the workout after that, and I saw real terror in Paul's eyes. The sweating and heavy breathing. On either side of him were the women, and I witnessed Paul squinting to see their asses as best he could when they went down to their push-ups. He is more obsessed with fawning over fat backsides and sturdy thighs than with pushing his lungs to capacity. After the workout, he went home and ate dinner and went to bed.

Paul at a chair that faces a desk, not writing but rubbing his head, wishing for more hair, bemoaning his lot as a guy who doesn't have enough social media followers, which brings me to my big news. My next novel is being published. This morning I announced it and received twenty-three thousand new followers who have scoured my timeline and retweeted old tweets I thought were genius. Now I am validated. My new agent said the publisher is "really so excited," as they suspect my first novel is going to sell very solidly. They are calling it that because, as they told me, "self-published novels are trash." I took no offense. Paul is about to self-publish his fourth self-published book, and that is so sad. The name of mine is *Dead, Lift*, and they are going to market it as a modern *A Sport and a Pastime*. An excerpt:

> The wailing of sirens, of police and ambulance. Red blue glittering on the acres of windows below. She rustled. Not yet morning. Maybe there had been a death. We did not pay attention to the end of things. Only life.
>
> "What do you think of the moon?" I asked, reaching out. I touched her ass. On the balcony hours earlier I put her fresh tits over the railing and pinched her nipples. She said, without fear I cannot come. The cool breeze bracing her body into immorality. I held her with one hand while the other pulled her hair, the pendulation, my hips slapping her bottom. Undone from my punishment, sleep came for her like a drowning. She was below the earth, but rising.
>
> "What do you think of the moon?" I asked again, trying to lift her. I could smell the smell of a woman, perfume and her ass, her shampoo. Her

hair all wild and curly and dark against my white pillow. The blueness in the room from the lunar cycle. She started to rustle.

"What do you think of the moon?" I asked a third time.

"The moon," she said, "is a beautiful thing God gave us." I did not think she believed. Maybe in her dreams she found Him, or He found her. I almost felt bad rousing her, distracting her from the spiritual awakening.

"God gave us many beautiful things," I replied, and did believe in Him at that moment. What he gave us was supernatural. Only the best could be known, or felt, or seen, like being inside the first spark of life, all warm and concentrated.

Or was it more like an atom? Forever contracting and expanding. My lover from the box could dead-lift a small truck, with hamstrings like cable wires, and seemed to have an endless capacity to give and receive, but she also was a painter. She had came over to my condo in the sky wearing nothing but yoga pants and a pink shag coat, her purple Nike Air Maxes. Her hair not done, she took off her coat and covered her pert teardrops. Powdered, she walked over to where she knew the liquor to be and made herself a neat Scotch. She did not turn. I knelt behind her and looked up to the heavens. She put her hands up against the wall and gasped for air.

"God gave us many beautiful things," she murmured, heading back to sleep.

Turning toward the moon, I imagined her speaking with God. Back on earth, she rubbed herself into my crotch, and I heard Him speaking. My Savior. Below us the sound of sirens. Death. A world turning. Only life.

A few days later I headed out to my balcony, climbed up on the railing and did handstand push-ups before falling backward, flipping to the ground and splattering. In the next moment I appeared again in the same spot. I had attempted to know death so as to try and understand Paul, who doesn't cry. He stares into the middle distance as he thinks about the trivial matter bothering him that day, something he said on Twitter is making him guilty or something he didn't say on Twitter is making him regretful, or he is rehashing a part of his commute that didn't go as he wanted, maybe a car followed him too closely or he perceived himself pulling out in front of another car, or maybe he is thinking about how fat he is after years of working out, or a combination of all that, instead of doing anything about any of his problems, like a guy who owns boxes would do. All that is boring. Let me tell you the story of how I found the agent who is going to pimp *Dead, Lift*. A few days ago I received an email from someone who said she'd read my first novel, *The Box*, and loved it.

"I couldn't believe how little attention it received," she wrote. She had family in Chicago and would be visiting them over the holidays. She asked if I wanted to come down, or she could even come up, if time allowed. We'd discuss my work, both future and past, "over a coffee, or even a drink. :)"

Arriving with a bottle of Pappy Van Winkle in nothing but a trench coat, my agent got me drunk and signed me to a contract entitling her to represent me for the next five novels. I didn't care if she signed me for a lifetime. She gave the best head I'd known since Seattle, when I met someone from Craigslist who worked at a bike store. On our first date we got pho but on our second we bought wine and went to the library to pick up the Émile Durkheim book on suicide she'd put on hold. We went to her place and drank in her gazebo in the cold spring. We went inside after we spotted a raccoon and put *Suspiria* in her laptop. I touched the inside of her healthy thigh, soft from never working out, over her white tights. She had a sensitivity such that the slightest touch made her posture slack, and from there we tumbled downstairs, and in her messy bedroom I received the greatest feeling I have ever known, and I knew I would have to say, if asked, "Some are better than others. I was once in the basement of this girl who worked at a bike store. I met her on Craigslist in Seattle and she had meaty thighs and a mouth that somehow elicited new sensations, as if she were working with a canvas other painters didn't have access to. She created new colors and vistas I never thought possible, and she did so knowingly, since she later said to me, when in one of her crying states, 'What am I, just a heavy girl who gives great blow jobs?' and she took it to heart when men said things in the heat of the moment that ranked her above the rest."

The agent from Chicago came over and sucked me so dry I thought I would never be able to regenerate again, as if she had pulled the DNA out of me, swallowing so deftly I could never suffer another defeat so overwhelming, as if it were a great honor to be so bested, like by an army led by a Napoleon or a Genghis Khan. My soldiers thought the same with the thick biker from Seattle, and now with the agent who lived in Manhattan but drove up from Chicago. If her love for my novel had anything to do with her acumen or vigor, I didn't ask, though she did state, unprovoked, "I love your prose, you fucking horse. God I love this cock."

I assumed she had used similar tactics with other men leading up to me—it'd be impossible to be that good on a first try, like becoming Michael Jordan your first time playing basketball—though with the others it wouldn't have been their writing but how much money they made. She usually dated men in finance, she said. Her wardrobe confirmed that, judging from what she dressed in after she came out of the shower, so fresh and red-cheeked on her ass, her silken hair still wet, her body swaddled in a white towel. She wrung out the water as she told me about her plans to get my novel sold. She asked me questions about what I planned to write next.

"Maybe about you and me," I said.

"You better fucking not," she said, putting on her thong, then slate-gray slacks and a black bra, a pink blouse, a slate-gray blazer, and finally black high heels. I asked her where she was going and she said she wasn't going back to Chicago but back to New York to get to work. For a goodbye she gave another rousing at my door, with morning light on her face, and when it was done I almost fainted. She sat me down. Gave me a glass of water.

"Drink," she said like Mary Magdalene. "Drink and be well." She caressed my thick hair. I feel asleep, maybe even before she left the building.

Back in my youth, I am remembering now, I lived in Seattle and played video games and drank too much and took air from those who deserved to breathe, but I was able to be with two girls at the same time. That's what *Dead, Lift* is also about, the erotic interplay of a decaying man who finds meaning in the flesh of two former Christians—one redheaded and one sandy blonde—who emerged from the rigidity of the church and found solace in ecumenical viewpoints which permitted vices like drinking too much wine and engulfing members. The main character is a drifting, prototypi-cal everyman who can't seem to find an anchor, jumping from one woman to the next, hoping they'll prop him up. There is also meta-phor, because every day on his way to his terrible day job he passes by a gym, and through the window he sees folks striving for some-thing he can't quite make out yet but knows somehow is meant for him. The two Christian girls in their late twenties, both of whom in the past have been romantically involved with Peter, the main char-acter, ask for a roommate, and that's where the real trilemma, as C. S. Lewis called it, begins. Does Peter fall into a steady relationship with Jenny, his longtime friend with benefits? Or does he branch out and try to start again with Hannah, a woman he saw for a month years before, who recently got out of a relationship?

I imagine the film version doing better in France, where they'll take the sex scenes and film them on a stage, just Jenny and Hannah experimenting. The novel is based on my time living in the base-ment of a woman from Craigslist, where I slowly deteriorated in a small bedroom connected to a hallway that had a washer and dryer and a bar the lady upstairs must have used once upon a time but hadn't in years, judging by the dust on the glasses, then a door that led up concrete stairs to the backyard, with a wooden fence and a gazebo, which housed a hot tub that would have been so nice, back when the bar was used, but neither was available while I lived there, even though the main selling point of the place had been that I could use the hot tub whenever I liked—she bait-and-switched by telling me when I moved in that she would look into how much it would cost to turn it on, but that would mean the rent would go up—and there were the bookcases in the other room she said she would move but never did and the crusty lamp and the clunky treadmill and the perpetually unlit brick fireplace, which she said on my first day there, seconds after she'd gotten her deposit check, I also could not use. I can't seem to scrape together enough memories now to remember why I had been so stupid as to live there. It must have been that I had to move and wanted to live alone. Still living with roommates and nearing thirty just seemed wrong. I didn't make much money working for UPS, so my landlady, who played online fantasy role-playing games at all hours of the day and night and advertised my basement room as a whole apartment with a hot tub, would have to do. I did not tell my parents everything, just that I had moved closer to work, and lived by myself now. I hoped to relieve their fears about the hippy-dippiness of my previous living arrangements. Things got better when Hannah and Jenny said they needed a roommate, and as soon as I could I was out of that basement with the unused bar and fireplace and hot tub and in the cozy environs of what they called "The Nest."

In years since first moving from the Midwest to Seattle I had grown heavier and lost hair. I worked in package delivery and each night Jenny and Hannah and I would "get tight" on the L-shaped couch upstairs to watch a British television comedy as we drank cheap wine from the nearby Grocery Outlet, nibbling on oven-warmed cheese sticks or nachos or brie with crackers. They'd draw even closer as the alcohol seeped into our pores. They believed in the sanctifying power of the blood of Christ, but they yearned to be touched, for their bodies to be worshipped and debased. I'd put one hand between Jenny's legs or Hannah's and feel my prick get harder as one or the other smirked or ever so slightly shut her eyes. I'd be careful, choosing louder portions of the show, so as not to cue the other, though I think they knew. Hannah was a forceful redhead and often returned the favor, sliding her long fingers under the blanket, inching her way under my waistband until she grabbed on and rubbed my slippery prick's head. One time, after Jenny went to the bathroom, she even showed me before she licked her fingers. Jenny would jack me off as coyly as she could, too, without rustling the blankets. One night after enough wine, or maybe I was getting bored, I occupied both of my hands. I know that's not mind-blowing to a lot of people, and to myself now, who has experienced every position with so many, but back then, as someone who was over-weight and could hardly afford to live in a bait-and-switch basement and who drank to forget, working my hands through tufts of hair—they used a compost bin to recycle their eggshells and wore sweaters instead of using heat in the winter and rode bicycles—was the most amazing thing I had experienced since kissing Maeve Kaufman's bare breasts the summer of our seventeenth year.

I spent nights with Jenny, who had tattooed crosses on the insides of her wrists. She maintained a more considerable bush as she was even more of a hippie than Hannah. She'd try to give me head but she used too much of her teeth, so I'd take her by the shoulders and sit her down on my prick and it didn't take long, her huge breasts bouncing in her lamplit room. I made a point afterward to try not to kiss, as I knew in the morning I'd be going to Hannah's room after Jenny left early to go build houses. I'd tiptoe in, and Hannah would giggle. She'd wave me into her welcoming bed and I'd kiss her wonderfully plain face and make her come quickly with my hand until she shook like someone having a seizure, then she'd watch as I spurted on her porcelain tummy. She'd giggle again, and say, "Oh Derrick," then get up to go to work. I'd fall back to sleep until I had to get up and go to work at the package delivery company in the afternoon. I'd get home late in the evening, and we'd do it all over again.

But, however great it was, being with those post-religious women with their thick bushes always left me empty, as if we were doing a prerecorded dance, like I had parts and they had parts. And while there was a basic appeal to that, I wanted more. I wanted to select from every woman on earth who would suck my prick dry, not just the ones I happened to live with and fell into bed with because our hormones told us to. I loved the Christian hippies, how they sinned and at the same time believed they were going to heaven. I did not want to dissuade them from that. I just wanted to move on to those who didn't think something better came later. I wanted the best of everything now. So I moved back to the Midwest and lost weight and purchased boxes and today I have a half-Asian half-Jewish book agent who wants me, and the novel with the movie on the way, and everything else.

But there is still the problem of Paul wanting to kill me, or have me killed, or I am going to die before this is all over. It's true that a murder would be the best, albeit cheapest, way to insert drama into these selfish inner ramblings. Considering the drama unfolding every day in the real world, there cannot be a more unsellable book, but that makes it exactly the kind of thing Paul would write.

As an example, yesterday while I lay in bed drinking A.H. Hirsch Reserve watching my agent scissor with another author she'd recently signed—a grad student from Iowa who posts pictures on Instagram of her backside with head-scratching captions like "Storms out, Butts out" and who is now signed on to write a trilogy of fantasy novels she self-describes as "subversive"—my mind started to drift from what unfolded in front of me, two bodies sliding off each other like eels, and I remembered, though it had never struck me before, that I once set fire to a school and got away with it, and because of this I would have to be punished, and I would be punished by dying in a mass shooting. How poetic, to die that way: after the last many years of celebrating life, to perish at the hands of those who exalt death. My creator would plant the insidious seed I am going to die by the hands of those whose main motive in life is killing, so that once they perish they will be given virgins to have their way with for eternity. It might be the most non-feminist idea in the world, and yet most feminists defend the barbarians for fear of seeming racist. How backward we have become, sleepwalking into oblivion, since the ones who do not believe in regressive sorcery do not make as many children, and the ones who do put their pricks in anything that moves, including family members, as long as they are of age, and that means anyone who has had her period. We are damned.

My agent and I argued about all this after I pulled the red-headed fantasy author's hair, yanking her neck. She wanted her face slapped hard enough that it left a mark. She liked me to throat-fuck her until she was gagging and spitting up. All that kind of stuff is fine, I guess. I like taking a woman from behind, holding her hands behind her as the smell of her ass fills the air from our workout, whose Lululemon yoga pants are around her ankles but whose strappy Lycra top is still on, and her tits are out and I am smacking my hips against her, with the stars out over the lake and the moon too, with people walking on the sidewalk below who dream of being with someone as attractive as her, yes I love all of that, then coming on her face as drops fall to the earth and she licks the rest away as if she has barbeque sauce on her cheek. All of that I am experienced in. But those more intense romps are always prodded by those who project a front aligned with the hard left, and I suspect the redhead and my agent project that persona online so as to gain more status. Still, I cannot blame them for deceiving others to make money. Either you are a child and think this world is fair or you are a realist.

We are not living in a cave in the mountains of Colorado, and I do not own a railroad. I am an owner of boxes, and after finishing with my agent and her author, after we had discussed the problem of religious terrorism, they smoked weed and watched *Playtime*. I was gawking at their bodies, also dumbfounded that *Playtime* could exist, or that any art could. My agent said it perfectly, between kissing the fantasy author's nipple absently: "Like, do you ever think about how difficult it must have been to make this? I mean, Jesus."

The fantasy author nodded, the drugs elevating my appreciation for the dedication necessary to complete the film, and that got me thinking more as I left my bedroom, passing the rows of vinyl records like in the movies about aging white men but less grungy and depressing, about how hard it is to make a new creation. It got even more confounding as I took out Prince's *Sign o' the Times*. He had to come up with the words and the drums and the guitar parts, and in that moment I grasped how incredible it was, the ineffable process of creation. Then the thought eroded and the nagging worm in my brain returned, the fear of being killed. I drank milk from the carton in my gleaming kitchen, and everything I'd worked for, all the comforts and erotic joys I enjoyed, I saw being snuffed out because a man who grew up poor and was taught to hate the Jews and the West and centuries-old sorcery thinks the best thing about this life is dying so that he can bed twelve-year-old virgins in the clouds for the rest of time. He would shoot me with a machine gun that could have never been conceived of in the time that most religions were formed. It was just too much. I needed to get it off my mind.

I got dressed, left the fantasy author and her agent, and went to work out down the street at one of my boxes. There I was greeted like a god. Many of the women blushed, remembering being a block away and up so many floors with their hands pressed against the glass and their yoga pants around their ankles and their sweaty backsides satisfied, and yet, despite their flushed faces and coy batting of eyelashes, I was sick with fear, thinking that any second someone would rush into the building shouting and shooting wantonly. The sensation did not abate for the whole workout, and I was ready to acquiesce to my ending when I noticed a young woman I had never seen before doing her push presses. Each time the bar shot in the air, her backside protruded from her so subtly and wonderfully. She turned a switch on inside me and I wanted to live. If the barbarians didn't kill me, I vowed in the middle of my WOD I would champion life, with her, if God willed it, or with anyone else who also knew that life is short and fragile and we should cherish it, no matter what, even if someone is out there penciling the blueprint for your demise.

There are antelopes in need of a safe space, and if we granted them that space what would the lions eat? No, you see, we can't. Unless we evolve past natural disasters and disease and nuclear war and drone strikes and people who strap bombs to their chest, there can be no safe spaces. We have to live knowing that at any time we could step outside and that could be it. Or even if you stay inside, a plane could run into your building, or if you live underground, an earthquake could swallow you whole. Or even if we did somehow transcend this terra, permeate the firmament and blast off to another planet, to a place where we all live off of Soylent and never have to work because we live in hovering clear pods suspended in the sky and the main job is to have a robot suck our genitals, we would not be guaranteed safety, because a star could slam into our new planet, or one of the robots could malfunction and bite our genitals off, or suddenly the universe could expand too quickly and we'd all become vapor. So while I'd like to tell Paul to carve out a safe space for me and everyone else, like at a campus where the students demand the best four years of their lives, pregnant with continual ideal scenarios, I know he couldn't do it, even if he wanted.

I woke with the dread. Last night after the box I took home the one doing push presses. She wore a sherbet-colored top with no sleeves, workout pants, impossibly tight black ones with matte black spots, and shoes with extra cushion, making her taller and her ass even higher. She read a chapter of my new novel while I sucked on her toes, and after that she modeled in the blue light from the moon in my condo with the floor-to-ceiling windows. I could have watched until the morning, the way the cut of her undergarments made her curves soar. I put her hands on the glass—my maid must wonder, when she comes in biweekly, why there are always smudges there—and she started to slowly move, like a deliberate hula dance, until I tore off the sweaty thong she'd worn to the box, and she yelped in helplessness, changing her voice, dipping or rising, and I said, "This pussy ain't safe here."

Warm in my bedroom afterward, she slept facedown without any covers. I wish I could give it its proper due. But I will fall short. Her backside was not so big it was gross, but it still almost seemed a genetic anomaly, the way it dominated her figure. I woke up, like I said, with the keen sense that I'd die, and I could do nothing to stop it. Why, though? I have, in the years that I've been aware of my existence, experienced good things, like the backside like a mound in my bed but I did struggle before I found success as a box and condo owner. I did yearn and work and sweat and bleed. My sins are that I am "douchey" or a "bro"? That's intolerant. I don't ever say all beta males in Portland deserve death. They put on their tight shorts one leg at a time, and we are all part of the human race. We should bond together, not split apart. I looked over and patted the ass. She woke, smirking into her pillow. I then went out and made myself a bloody mary and stood out on my balcony. Down in the lake fish swam by, waving their tails, nibbling on algae in the dark or eating other swimmers. They went about their day like nothing, not aware that other fish could be even larger and eat them and in an instant they could no longer be. All of this is so trivial, yet I want to live. Am I more important than a fish? Right as I thought that, down below I saw a van pull up, and men streamed out of it wearing camouflage balaclavas. Around their chests were bandoliers strapped with ammunition. There must have been ten, all shouting in Arabic.

I ran downstairs and met the men in the stairwell who yelled at me about meeting up in Dabiq. But with the calm assurance there were virgins on earth, they relented and promised to go home, infused with a newfound appreciation for not murdering. They promised to convert their families to seek a road of reformation that will inform a generation that rises up and topples theocracies and supplants governments with the tools needed to provide the populace with education and basic rights, no matter their beliefs, ensuring a state where it is encouraged to speak one's mind on any topic at any time without fear of corporal punishment. After we shook hands and they left I had the desire for women to put their fingers in my butt, and mine obliged after I ate her ass to calm her nerves. At the door I slapped her juicy apple, imprinting its shape on my mind, and she had that look in her eyes that said she wanted to stay and would text me very soon. Once she left I put on Nike sweatpants, along with a camel-colored cardigan and a plunging v-neck, and a gold cross around my neck, reaching down to the tattoos near my clavicle, then white Converse and a gold watch, and I walked into the gray city, a star among the beer-addled citizens, for a leisurely trip to the bookstore so as to get a grasp on my competition. On my way I was honked at by a group of girls driving to the UWM campus. They pulled to a rolling stop and leered, asked if I needed a ride.

"Tempting," I said. "Maybe another time."

As they drove off one of them yelled out her open window, "I'd fuck your brains out, bro!" She was the most rambunctious of the four, itching to take her turn punishing my body for sins she and her friends would make up on the fly. I kept going, unmolested for the last few blocks, except for the stares.

Just inside the bookstore and to my right there was a series of posters advertising readings by novelists and short-story writers and a few nonfiction types. They were muted-looking, with openings to their books like, "We were traveling down worn roads, at a crossroads, our hearts burdened with regret." The majority were younger women who wrote not-so-vaguely autobiographical novels about what it was like to have college friends they don't talk to anymore and now things are different because they have husbands who work at jobs and a child and they feel overwhelmed by that and sometimes they imagine what it might be like to have sex with other men. The outliers wrote science-fiction stories that were real-life stories, all of them guys in their late thirties who idolized George Saunders and hoped to one day bed their graduate students.

Past the posters I experienced a sudden twitch, like I needed to vomit, and the only medicine could be the flesh of the pasty writers on the wall, the only manna that could sustain me as I staggered in and sat down by the Suggested Reads section. On a padded bench I thumbed through a bad novel, like almost all the rest, and soon fell into a deep sleep. Hours later I woke and found I could not move, my ankles tied to bedposts, my arms bound. I could hear talking and laughing, the sound of dubstep thumping throughout the house. The murmur of a party, dancing and happy shouting. The smell of weed. The room I had been chained inside was serene, a lamp on, clean, with everything in order. A jewelry box on the dresser and an acoustic guitar propped in the corner. A framed Klimt poster on the wall. I imagined colored thong underwear in the drawers, and small jean shorts. Long sweaters and oversized coats in the closet. I fell back asleep and when I woke the four girls from the car—I don't suppose I can call them women if they were at the age where you take Psychology 101—surrounded me. They had kidnapped me from the bookstore while I slept, utilizing a *Weekend at Bernie's* ruse to escape detection, they said. They were nude. One started at my feet, her pure clean ass toward me, and her friend joined her. Another bent down and faced away as she started to ride me, while the last one strolled over and sat on my face, grinding herself in so the flesh flipped and softly pinched my nose and lips. When they had finished and finished me they told me they couldn't wait to read my novel. We slept in the same bed. In the morning, they said, we'll untie you.

I walked home sore, four new numbers in my phone with accompanying nude avatars. On the walk I thought about my soon-to-be-released novel and how nobody cares about fiction but about immigration policies and the loss of culture and sexism in video games and how much water is consumed by a cow to produce one hamburger and overpopulation and religious extremism and mental health and the accessibility of assault rifles and black-on-black murder and white privilege and whether black-on-black murder is a result of white privilege and whether white privilege is a result of people being online too much and all the bees dying and butt sizes and online followers and body mass index and if calories are even a useful metric anymore and if someone is really as happy as they are on their social media page and who knows the proper networked individuals in their selected field and the militarization of police and the senseless deaths in the streets and people going to jail for a little weed and other people not going to jail for murder and diseases carried by mosquitoes that could wipe all of us out in a couple months and who is going to be president of this stretch of land and who is racist and who is not racist and opioid addiction and ethics in listicle journalism and who is retweeting whom and if we are using "who" and "whom" the right way and why didn't I get retweeted and monogamy is outdated and am I going to die alone?

Luckily there was money coming in from my box franchises, so even if my novel doesn't sell I'll still be able to live in the sky and sleep on Egyptian cotton and step on heated tiles and bed yoga instructors. Yet I have to admit, as I walked away from the college campus, past retirement homes on Prospect, and saw my condo jutting up on the skyline, I was disheartened to think that my greatest artistic achievement could go by without anyone noticing, that I'd spent so much time on *The Box* and *Dead, Lift*, and the most I could hope for was that a boyfriend waiting for his girlfriend to finish shopping at Zara would go into one of the last remaining bookstores, find his way past the magazines and board games and picture books and vinyl records and calendars, and see my novel tucked in among titles representing hundreds of thousands of hours spent alone in a room, and at best that man is interested enough, after seeing the cover and scanning the description, to flip it open, and maybe he appreciates the first paragraph and considers for a second buying it, before his girlfriend texts him a picture of herself in the dressing room, and she normally never does that—she meant to send it to someone else—so he rushes out to give her more money so she can buy more clothes.

I told my half-Asian half-Jewish agent about this problem, and she told me not to worry. She came over when I got back to my condo after the college girls had taken me captive, bringing with her the red-haired fantasy author as a book release present. I welcomed them with fine cheeses and wines from the Whole Foods only two blocks away. My agent knows I like it when she goes into a parody, and she said it like this, as the fantasy author began to take off her clothes, her tits buoyant upon release from her black bra: "Oh no, you-a no worry, you-a-like what we do now." She wore white Kabuki paint, with the red lipstick, while the fantasy author wore the dark eye makeup redheads wear. She kissed me as my agent went down lower. I put one hand on the back of her head and the other between the redhead's legs. There was smoothness, as if she had just gone to the salon.

"That's nice," I whispered. "You should stay in Milwaukee and I'll watch it grow. I would tend to that fucking garden so good."

I wasn't making sense. The head and ass-eating made my mind a worthless jelly. I could hear them working as I looked out at the lake and managed to have the thought, What if I become a full-time fiction writer? What if I sell all my boxes? Take a chance and start over and see if I can have another chapter? Later, as my agent sat on my prick and the fantasy author sat on my face and swiveled her hips, I was almost forty years old. Shortly after, while I was in the fantasy author's ass and she squealed, or maybe it was how my agent sprayed wildly, I was sure I could change people's minds about fiction. Women with tattoos and tasteful landing strips and big sexy noses are the ones I'll start with, I thought, as my agent and the fantasy author slept in a coma. The world is ready.

And now Paul speaks...

...How do I explain?

I woke, checked my phone—I am a robot like everyone else—and saw an email. This was rare for me, outside of Twitter telling me to follow someone or Xbox wanting me to come back to their Gold subscription or, really, that's about it. My wife used to email me from work, but those were always about a fight, and now we don't even have the energy for that. First thing in the morning, since I can never sleep late, with my mind racing as it does the second it enters consciousness, mulling over every worry, I saw the email. There was a time when I received notifications from online dating websites, or when I wrote for Thought Catalog I'd get a new follower or so for every article I wrote, but that's years ago now and my email account has dried up. Still I check it obsessively, as if I am suddenly going to receive the message that will change my life. So I rolled over in the bed and touched the mail button, like I do every morning, expecting nothing, and also everything, somehow, and

I saw a message from someone named Derrick. I assumed it was spam, but after the sleep wore off and I could refocus, I realized he was addressing me:

> Bro, my novel is being published today, and I want to tell you I'm selling all my boxes, with or without your permission, and am going to become known as a novelist, just like you always dreamed you'd be but never could. Don't fap so much; I see you.
> xoxo,
> Derrick

I clicked on the link this Derrick person had sent, and his Amazon page seemed real. But he was a tool, doing his best to masquerade as an artist. Not that every artist doesn't do that, but Derrick looked like he had been taking steroids. Someone draped a sweater on him and slicked back his hair, though no need on the shaved sides, and plopped on generic black-rimmed glasses that screamed youth pastor. From the preview I read, the protagonist in the novel Derrick wrote worked as a CrossFit instructor and owned several "boxes," or gyms, and from the first few pages I read it seemed like he just goes around having sex with well-formed college girls who practice yoga. It didn't sound like a terrible life, even if it was hollow, but empty isn't all bad. I once tried to fill my life with meaning and look at me: paralyzed, unhappy, my wife even more so. I left my writing aspirations behind in my early thirties, after I never got an MFA and could never manage to attract a following online, never producing traction through buzzworthy content so that molesters would validate me and push me up to the front of the crowded lit raft where The One in charge could see me well enough to examine my work and evaluate whether or not I could be someone they chose to become part of The Club, where everyone inside gets the benefit of the masses propping them up through the meager donations that collectively gird the wobbly scaffolding that is The Scene: writing articles for money, landing grants, getting book deals, et cetera and so on.

Saying et cetera and so on is redundant, I know, and yet I wrote it anyway, which serves as a good example of why I never made it, along with the obvious reasons: not having good hair and not living in New York City. As an INFJ psychic born on the second of July I knew I would never become known, but I pressed on nonetheless. I had stories to tell, and they taught us in elementary school in the '80s that if you do something long enough and try hard and keep saying your dream out loud you'll make it. As I got older and heard variations of that vacuous aphorism spouted by people who'd gotten lucky—and had great hair and lived in New York City—I knew they were lying. They spoke out of obligation to some invisible master that all successful people want to worship. They don't believe in God but want to be grateful to Someone. I kept going, and going, and going, in teeth-grinding, chalky determination to not have worked at a thing for so long for nothing.

Now here I am, every day going to a bad job with awful people, gaining weight and losing hair, and I woke up this morning and saw an email. Derrick must have meant to send it to another Paul, someone who once doubted him and now is getting told what the what is. I can sympathize. If I were in Derrick's shoes and fortunate enough to have a novel released, not self-published, and people other than myself cared if it sold or not, fussed over it—if there were storyboards, and meetings about the cover, and emails sent back and forth between managers and the marketing department, and an advertising budget was allocated, and royalties were assigned numbers by lawyers, and one of the lawyers was attractive with an ass other people commented on for its size and athletic stature when she wore certain pantsuits in the office, and she wanted to be with me based solely on one reading of my book—well, then I'd have the kind of confidence that might drive me to send an email like the one I received this morning, and more after that, to others who have done me wrong.

And now Derrick speaks again…

…An email might shake him up a little bit, is what I thought. I'd tired of him staring into the abyss. His eyes are what make up my walls and the moon, the grass and the streets below, the women who put their hands on my windows and leave streaks, the boxes I own. He is woven through the fabric of all reality but uncaring. I thought if I could get in touch, I might jolt him. But he took the most predictable route and chose the path of least resistance. He deleted the email and went back to his day of worrying. In happier news, my novel came out today, and the early reviews are in from *The Millions*, *McSweeney's*, and even my agent's mom at the Times. All are resoundingly positive. Bookslut called it "…an empowering novel that is also debasing. An accomplishment." Lit Hub said, "…the prose is strangely hypnotic, as if lulling us into a trance of erotic pleasures, those unknown to regular society in their missionary positions with worn-out OkCupid girlfriends who screech about hashtags. The anti-modernity modern novel that will blow you away." Jezebel even reviewed it, saying, "If fucking the author of this book means setting back the women's movement, I'll happily give up my right to vote."

My agent also said there is going to be an HBO series, and with that will come the features on TMZ and regular appearances on *Extra*, and from there summers in Provence, assuming Europe still exists in a few summers. Drinks with Drake. Maybe I'll start a modern-day Brat Pack filled with painters and models. All of this is happening now, so I hope Paul stays away.

"Keep out of my life," I yelled from my balcony. My neighbors below me, who exist though I have never seen them, must think I'm crazy. For all I know they're specters, with half-formed faces that wouldn't appear unless I went to them now, and even then they'd only be recognizable by their most prominent features, like the wife has acne and the husband is skinny but "boasts a protruding gut from drinking too much, judging by their racks of wine, visible as I walked in."

Shouting seems to have helped. Paul stopped trying to write and went back to talking to himself about mundane things, like if he should reset the internet for the ten thousandth time or break down and call the cable company or cancel the service altogether. Right as he stopped typing, my phone began to light up with praise. And to see it ping whenever another stranger hopped online to suckle at my genius, how great. I had made a way for myself; what had Paul done? He had not created anything but the world I live in, which is gray and dour. Any brightness is what I brought by bedding yoga babes in their early twenties with thick thighs. Meanwhile Paul sulks because earlier today, when he couldn't pronounce a last name, his boss had said that men are terrible at reading and spelling, and Paul once thought he could be a writer. He wanted to specialize in the arts, and there he was fumbling over last names so his boss could cross them off a list. She, a woman in her forties who loves the Packers and playing with her pet Chihuahuas, could tell him, a guy who once wanted to be listed among thinkers in the *Paris Review*, that he was wrong about the pronunciation of a word, and by extension he wasn't smarter than someone who ate Burger King for breakfast every morning and whose favorite place in the world was Potawatomi Casino

By the way, my book sales are incredible. I didn't even think people bought novels anymore, but they must, because *Dead, Lift*, about a man who comes back from the dead to save a group of ailing CrossFitters stranded on an island, has become a "nationwide sensation," as Mimi, my half-Asian half-Jewish book agent, told me. She always throws her hair to one side. I love that. I also love her passion for promoting my work and giving me pleasure. There is a book tour, and both she and the red-haired fantasy author with the devastating mons pubis—she always wears high-waisted pants or workout clothes and you can see that it is fatty and lovely, or maybe it's only that way when she's around me and the veins are sending blood down to her—are coming along. Tomorrow it starts, and I can't wait. I imagine Paul in the coming weeks, working at a job in a cubicle, struggling with his weight, worrying about the bags under his eyes, resenting his boss and pretending to write when really he is playing computer games, all the while getting further away from the debate swirling online about race and presidents and refugees and being racist and everything else that is important to comment on if you want to be relevant. He will grow older and fatter and I will stay the same age, and slay pussy and get money.

We started in San Francisco and packed City Lights, then up to Portland, where we showed up at Powell's like the Beatles. From there we took a private jet to Seattle, to Elliott Bay Books. I touched hands in the crowd as if healing them. Then to Minneapolis, to Magers & Quinn, where graduate students came as soon as they saw me, as if I had hooked them all to the same erotic wire. They threw at me what remained of their Stafford loans, as if it were Monopoly money. They took off their parkas and exposed their white breasts. From the outline of a bikini, I could tell one of them had been to Hawaii or Mexico. I told her the next morning that was why I'd picked her. She begged me to take up residency at her university, saying her dad was the head of the English department. I just continued eating out her prim ass. Madison was a blur. "I fear I may have a sex addiction," I said from the podium, and every-one laughed, but I was proven correct. There were six that night. Chicago was dirty and New York City even dirtier but I loved it. The last stop was in my home city of Milwaukee, at Boswell Books, less than a mile from my condo where I have been with many Asian and redheads, Jews too, all of them yelping as their faces mashed against the floor-to-ceiling windows. I was less than a mile from there in the bookstore, reading from my new novel. I saw the women from the last years seated in the metal folding chairs. This was their chance to shout that I was a jerk and hadn't called them back, that I was a misogynist who made up lies about the duration of our acts. Not one called out. They sat in the audience wearing their best outfits and in full makeup and dress, scanning to see which "heifer," as they said in their mind, had been with me. Rolling their eyes, they imagined what kind of "fucking ridiculous yelping that bitch did." After the reading they asked questions, inquiring about my process, but I cut them off at fifteen minutes. I was tired from the tour and snuck out the back. I walked down Prospect where it was quiet and peaceful for blocks. I did not see another soul until near the end, when a lady walking her dog looked at me. It was Paul. A black man on the phone. A baby in the stroller. Paul. Paul. I ran the rest of the way home, not looking at anyone, managing to make it to the elevator, where a toddler jumped in and pressed the emergency button. There was nothing to do. I kneeled down and the little tyke touched my head and I was transported, shown all sorts of terrors.

Now I'm back in my condo in the sky. After learning the horrors from the magical baby, I went back to the bookstore and gathered up as many fans as I could. With so many years of being alone, I now had the chance to have an orgy in my thirtieth-floor condo overlooking the most famous lake in America. So I took the opportunity to play my pipe and watched them all follow me like baby ducklings, their underwear becoming soaked as they walked, like when you walk on wet sandals, and in my condo I saw them take shots of high-end liquor from each other's belly buttons—something I once thought only happened in movies—and watched as they used advanced techniques like edging and hinting and surprise and consistency and rhythm and scissoring and accenting and multiples and framing and staging and layering and orbiting and signaling, transforming my condo into a NASA control room. I would have been crazy not to stand in awe. I drank triumphant drinks of wine and enjoyed the view, out beyond the flesh to the water, waves beating, my oars again rowing with the tide.

The next morning there were fit babes strewn on the couches and Eames chair and soft bed, the light barely creeping in, the automatic shades drawn. I made coffee, careful to fold the delicates on my counter. There were the boxes and the success with a wide swath of women, but before that there was great struggle, the kind I could write six or seven or eight long novels about, and people would read them, because now I was someone people wanted to read about and know how many struggles I'd had. The coffee percolated and I chuckled to myself, I used to fall in love. I thought it was a real thing and not a made-up word. At twenty-three I was a group-home worker and pathetic and now in my condo women were stacked on top of each other. I saw the sweet rise of their protruding tummies and heard one snore. She had a voracious appetite and spoke French. She put croissants and macaroons and delicious items in her mouth. She had a hunger. She'd said in my box that she chose Milwaukee because it seemed "the most American city, but not as big as Chicago." She had grown up in the country, north of Châtillon-sur-Seine, and had a tangy body odor that made her more alluring. She slept. They all did. None of them knowing after I was houseparent I fell in love with an Alabaman from MySpace, and that I had been so pathetic.

I tiptoed around two who work out at one of my boxes. If they are not sisters they are very good friends, always talking in high-pitched singsong about what classes they are taking at UWM or what kind of makeup they're buying. Their bodies are thick, and one of them has a square jaw, and she is so rounded in the back, with torpedoes for breasts. How could they be sisters, I thought, remembering what they had done the night before, re-creating a scene from an iconic film of the early 2000s by going back to back on all fours, the rest of us using our phones in the darkness as flashlights. I didn't tell them I once fell in love for a third time, with a Minnesotan teen in the Pacific Northwest, with curly hair and a long torso and a small bottom. For a long time I labored in regret over not holding on to her, until I moved away, just as I had moved away from the sculptor in Alabama, just as I had moved away from the Iowan volleyball player in Nebraska, a houseparent with an Olympian's body. After the Pacific Northwest, to Minneapolis, where I online dated. I fell over and over and over again, that's how it would have seemed to others, but looking back I know there was just one more, a rich girl from Connecticut. Twenty-three, with hairy armpits. She gave me a hand job on my mattress on the floor in the attic where I lived with my landlord downstairs, and another in the morning when we woke up. Her body odor was strong for someone with such refined tastes and an East Coast pedigree. She grew up going to summer camps that taught Thoreau and Singer. She was entitled and fought for the rights of those who could never be part of her tribe, unless they were already part of her tribe, and I was so pathetic.

I did not tell any of that to the one lying on my Eames chair, a girl who came to the gym with an Indian man normally, and I think it was her, with long legs and a tiny ass, who was probably the wildest of the whole bunch, flitting from my cock to the next available crotch like a hummingbird. I stepped over her and squeezed in next to a Jewish girl on my leather couch, there in the morning with my coffee. She put her head on my shoulder and her hand on my crotch, tapping it once and letting it rest there. Of all of them, I most had hoped she'd come to the reading. I even for a second thought of texting her to make sure she would, then thought better of it, knowing how pathetic I once was. I had been hugely relieved when I saw her sit down in the back row. She could be inconspicuous and still be noticed. I loved watching her exercise at my box. It was like breathing to her. She was not skinny, nor was she so muscular. She teetered on the edge, with defined arms and legs with meat but still womanly, and abs when she breathed heavily, and a big sexual nose and sleepy eyes and a smile that did not come often, and when it did it was just a smirk, saying *I know everything you are thinking. I know what everyone is thinking.*

She whispered in my ear, "I love your novel," and I was aroused and could tell she was, and soon, in staggered sections, the rest began to wake, like babies in a nursery who hear one cry and that makes all the rest of them cry. None of us shed tears. Someone opened the shades. The sun shined in Milwaukee.

And Paul speaks once more…
…I dreamed the other night that I published a novel and there was a reading at Boswell Books. All the women from my CrossFit class came. They dressed up, wore makeup, had their hair done. Some came in spandex, but most arrived in skirts and blouses, sweaters, boots or heels. Some in the front row spread their legs, like in *Basic*

Instinct, and gave me a view of everything, but I kept my composure and read from my novel, which had been optioned by a movie studio. When I finished they all came over, but I no longer lived where I lived near the worms. I lived in the towers, the palatial condos they built a few years ago, the most modern buildings on all of Prospect domineering the skyline and overlooking the lake, on the very top floor. They took up the living room and began to undress each other. When I woke in the morning in my real apartment on the ground, I kept the dream to myself. My wife slept beside me, restful after her late shift at the hospital.

And now Derrick speaks again...

... Today I am thinking of going out for pho, taking the Jewish girl with the ripped arms. I might have to tell my agent and the redheaded fantasy author we are now a foursome. They'll understand. Other big news is coming in even now: I've been asked to go to Hollywood to go over a script adapted from my novel. P.T. Anderson is directing and Adèle Exarchopoulos is playing the lead. Demi Lovato is costarring in her first feature film. Their youth and thickness and sturdy frames will fit the tone. I landed in California—palm trees, movie stars, cops on motorcycles—and met P.T. at his mansion "up in the hills," so we could do some storyboarding. P.T. and I sat down by his pool. A maid brought us drinks and we got down to it. P.T. had a grand vision for my work, like the view of Los Angeles from his pool.

"I have a grand vision for your work," said P.T., with the hills in front of us. In the middle of the day, looking over a dry desert with encroaching insecure thirsty humans who need attention to survive, I could see my name in lights. One day there would be a reality show about my family with me as the grandfather, more talked about than seen, as my descendants spread out like the stars as God promised Moses or Abraham or whoever it was, and they would all be very entitled. They wouldn't know any other way. I would have provided for them a life where they were always waited on, with bottles of water in sub-zero refrigerators blending in with the rest of the kitchen.

After brainstorming for a short time P.T. lined up rows of white powder. Time went by in a blur and we came up with more great ideas and soon enough darkness fell and important people like Amy Adams showed up. There was a bartender in a tuxedo, offering martinis from a circular tray. Topless women swam, many up-and-coming actresses not yet twenty-five, fondling each other's wet nipples in the warm pool. Half out of my mind on designer cocaine and good whiskey, I took my shorts off and a limp prick joined them. They giggled as they took turns tugging at me under the water. I swam down and heard only the murmur of the party above, and thought of my girls in Milwaukee. In California the women were small. It was good to see them nude and kissing, yes, but it was almost like they were a puff, like the weight of their wet swimsuit bottoms could drown them. My CrossFit girls were domineering, like Vikings. The girls in California would snicker at those Midwestern thick asses and muscular thighs and rippled backs, but deep down I knew they'd be jealous. I wanted to fly my Wisconsin girls all in at that moment.

Nothing happened, just more revelry. The gaunt actresses drinking and swimming. A couple of them chose me, and we put on sandals and found a dark area behind a cactus. But they made noises like the noises made by those who are paid to make noises, as if they were doing what they thought a man would want, not what came naturally, not letting it erupt out of them as my Milwaukee girls did, full of beer and squeaky cheese. Before I finished they ran back to the party, jumping back in the pool. I could hear them singing along to a song with the word "nigger" over and over, though the only black person at the party was one of the security guys on the other side of the house who looked like he could push-press a good-sized car. I passed out at some point, waking up to the hot sun on the baking concrete in midday, stumbling into the open-plan living room, where I found P.T. in a robe, watching a movie on his reel-to-reel. A few of the partiers remained, just scraps, mascara running down their eyes as they tiptoed away on the hot ground, carrying their heels. I said goodbye to P.T. and he waved without looking.

"I'll see you soon," he said, though I somehow knew he wouldn't.

Home again with a string of graduated beads gently slipped into my ass by a strong and calloused hand while the other reached under my balls to grab hold of my prick. She pulled with her lotioned hand on the ringed end of the beads, sliding them in and out, until I noticed myself moaning, and soon came all over the laundered bed sheets. They say the average single man changes his sheets less than five times a year. Mine are rotated and pressed every week. I was in a bed above Lake Michigan, the sinewy Jewish girl beside me. She liked satisfying me more than anything, and that was what had begun to grate on me about my agent. She'd coo and swim her legs in bed after I'd watched her finish three or four times. I'd told her that she could just do it herself, if she needed it that much, but I could never allay her desires, and her pleas would mess with my sleep, which is why I insisted she fly in less and work on selling my novel more. In just its third month *Dead, Lift* has sold over a half-million copies. Not since Salinger has the literary scene heaped such praise on a novel so commercially successful. The few odd detractors have been transparently jealous. After the emails and tweets and notifications and texts and requests for interviews and trips to Hollywood, it was nice to be back in Milwaukee having my butthole plundered by a strong Jew with a backside so good it's hard for me to believe it's real, connected to muscular thighs and sinewy arms and a sexual nose. She is the only one who seems to not want something from me. We were resting in bed.

"Tell me something about you from before I knew you," she said in her thong. She came just from watching me come. Her mons pubis was fat and perfect. Somehow her breasts stayed perked toward the skylight in my lofted ceiling.

"From before I knew you?" I asked.

"Yes."

"Why," I said quickly, "do you want to get married?" And I smirked to disguise the truth: that she was someone I could see myself marrying. Middle age on the horizon, my body slacked from being on the road. I'd sold my boxes and had so much money. She didn't care. She had her own means.

"I am married," she said. "I told you, didn't I?"

She might have, and I might have forgotten. Either way I was glad I had only entertained for a second the idea of getting married and being with only one. Even if at the start she said she was "sort of a lesbian" and didn't mind if her man "played with other women," or even joined in with her, I knew that when the wedding bells rang out and the rings were exchanged all that would turn out to be false advertising.

"I knew that," I said. "That's why I like you so much. I like thinking about you dreaming of my cock when you're with him. Do you?"

She touched on my limp prick. "Maybe, but I'll only let you know how much I really need it if you tell me something. Something nobody else knows."

And that is when it happened, when I became like a marionette. Paul pulled the strings, and I told my beauty a story about how when he lived in Minneapolis he came upon a man at the top of a wooden staircase, and just as he started up, as if it were timed for a scene in a movie, he toppled forward and fell to the bottom, then staggered over to a set of concrete stairs leading to an apartment building, but Paul didn't run over; he walked, wondering, thinkinkg, How could this be real? He tried to talk to the man, who seemed to be on drugs or drunk or homeless or a norm-core hipster.

"Like a Mac DeMarco," I said, "but quite a bit more disheveled and disoriented and surly."

Paul continued to speak through me, about how he picked up one of the lenses that had fallen out of the hobo's eyeglass frames, but the man just grunted, so Paul put it down and saw on the man's forehead a decent gash. The man's head lolled, and Paul nervously said through me to my one and only that he was anxious because he didn't know if he was supposed to call an ambulance or if the guy was all right and this kind of thing happened all the time, like maybe he was just a drunk local whose ass crack was showing. I was neutered. I didn't know what to do. No one was around. Would the man be angry if I called an ambulance? But he still wasn't responding or talking, so something was wrong.

"I had no guts at all," I said to my lover, who had slid out of bed in the middle of the story. "For the rest of my life," I said, "I will be guilty for not calling the ambulance, and that is one of the main reasons why I'm not a writer."

"But you are, no?" she said. She was up. She had put on her Lycra workout pants and teal-and-pink-cushioned tennis shoes.

"No, I'm not," I said.

"Well, that's too bad, but I have to get back to my husband," she said, and she left the bedroom. As the front door with the magnetic entry closed, I meekly said, "Okay."

The morning she left I returned from a labored run to find I was heavier than before. My tattoos gone, I became dispirited. I had been with Asians and redheads and Jews and yoga babes, but now I was run-down, bald and fat. I looked like a dad of twins who had a job with a mean boss who didn't let him go home on time and gave him the on-calls over holidays. I collapsed on my bed and began to wail. I had so many missed calls and texts about hooking up, but none from my meaty Jew. We were done. In a matter of minutes I had become one of the clingers of her past, a beta male, a social-justice warrior. The only thing left for me to do was jump from my condo in the sky. I could not remember not existing before I was born. I would not remember not existing after I died.

I walked out to the balcony and stood on the ledge, and just the day before I could have done a handstand and not fallen. I could have carefully set myself back on the solid ground. As a worthless blob of flesh I slimed off to one side and went tumbling to the ground. I died instantly and was reborn at the ledge. I got down.

There are so many rings around Saturn. We know so little about the universe. I have been with colors and persuasions, and they have put their fingers in my ass. I have written successful novels and met with a respected auteur in California. I have bought and sold boxes. I have lost weight and been chiseled. I am a normal person with anxieties and worries. I mess up everything.

Seattle Christmas, 2007

*B*efore the balding and double chins, before the self-doubt, before the temp jobs and online dating, I worked as a dispatcher at UPS in Seattle. Before getting the job, I didn't know anything about dispatching. All I'd done to qualify for the position was pass an Orwellian test that measured one's ability to parse what one "should do" versus what one "should not do" in rock-and-hard-place managerial scenarios. It seemed an elaborate setup for the test-taker to see if he or she would side with the management over the union. I had failed it back in Sioux Falls, but in Seattle I took it again and passed with flying colors. Once, don't ask me how, I heard a rumor that I hadn't missed one question. A month later a balding man came into the truck I was loading at about six in the morning---the big garage doors open, the sun not yet up over Mount Rainier---and offered me an interview. A week after that, in an office built like an interrogation room, I presented myself as a guy who could type fast and take orders. According to the balding manager who wisped over the last few strands God had cursed him with, those were the only qualifications.

While waiting to hear back I met new folks in the city. I was ready to break free of the restrictive youth that had bound me in the Midwest. Through the liberal church I attended for the first month or so in Fremont, I met a redhead who convulsed when she came and a sandy blonde with enviable breasts made all the more special by the fact that no one had ever touched them. I doubt even she did, except to wash them, and that was beautiful as well, as if seeing a Michelangelo painting not on the ceiling of the Sistine Chapel but on the walls of a cave in Afghanistan, where only lucky adventurers would happen upon the masterpiece. She was a shy girl from the Twin Cities who liked to paint birds and listen to ska, but the one I loved, who this is about, was a curly-haired girl, woman now, who I later realized may have been Jewish, the way her hair would take up a whole picture. She'd gone to Spain for her senior year of high school and smoked weed from her handmade bowl and gave such numbing head I think I once almost lost consciousness. All this from someone from northern Minnesota who laughed in a way that melted your cares. She could not always keep eye contact when she talked with me, for fear of turning red in the cheeks.

That summer for my twenty-seventh birthday, my parents came to visit. As the youngest in our family I had been coddled, but the time and money and attention put into me could not be prolonged much longer. My chances dwindled with each passing year and the unspoken expectation I might do something great shrunk. Inwardly I still believed I would do something great, even if so far all I'd been able to do was move away to a bigger city. Package distribution seemed as good a field as any to begin my climb. On the last day of my parents' visit, I remember, after taking them on long walks and shown my mom the areas she requested I take pictures of but never did, ordered them pho and given tutorials on how to use chopsticks, trudged up Queen Anne Hill for a view from Kerry Park, toured them around Elliott Bay Marina where I waxed boats—the early mornings were for package loading in SODO— we went to their hotel room in Tukwila near the airport, and they told me to invite my new friends. We were going to order pizza, swim in the outdoor pool, and instead of playing baseball, like in my youth, watch the Twins versus the Mariners on TV.

Great news had come that morning. The balding manager at UPS called and offered me the dispatcher job, and for the first time in my life I knew, instead of sensed, I'd make it. My parents, I think, even noticed, judging by how my mom looked at me as we ate a late breakfast in the hotel in a half circle of a booth, how my dad kept asking earnest questions about the position. In my head, I thought: I will not always be poor, not always alone. It had been my worry for as long as I could remember since I was never good at math and I went to the resource room for speech therapy. I remember being alone in college and physically aching as I pounded the mattress of my lofted bed, crying out to God as if I were in a black-and-white Swedish film, *When will I be given a girlfriend?* In high school Lacey and Stacey and another Lacey were not right. As that nearly twenty-year-old man, I needed a Jennifer, or a Rachel, or please God, I prayed, a Claire. Andrea from the big Christian meet-up group on campus came along and we made out in my dorm room with *The Matrix* on VHS in the background. We held hands in a gazebo as she talked of wounds from boys in the past, guys who wore Five Iron Frenzy patches on their jean jackets. Please God, Andrea, I prayed then, may she be The One. Her blonde hair, tan stomach. The belly-button ring when she wore her halter tops. She rode horses and when she tickled me I could tell she was strong from years of tending animals by the way her hands dug into my sides. I wanted to smell her hair and kiss her and read Bible verses with her until we died in our old ages and went to heaven. The last summer of college came and went, and in the fall I called Andrea for an update on the progress of our courtship. That's when she told me she was with another, a thirty-year-old with two kids. His name was Vance or Vince, I think now. Maybe Bill. Alone. Poor. Alone.

I was never good at math, like I said, so in college I chose psychology as my major. My soul, at the time, was too pure for advertising classes with the girls who wore black lace chokers, and I had too much pride to major in communications with the jocks. I earned my teaching license, even if teaching high school was the last thing in the world I wanted to do. For a month or so after I graduated college I substitute taught in my rural hometown, sinking as low as I thought I could, before I sank lower and began a full-time job in North Sioux City where they made Gateway computers. I'd been hired, with help from my sister who worked as a real teacher, as an in-school suspension supervisor. The job amounted to telling kids who'd been kicked out of their regular classrooms for not wanting to be told what to do what to do. An Indian girl who acted like a woman from the Upper East Side of New York City, a overweight kid with an Abercrombie & Fitch model for a brother, a sex-obsessed junior-high girl, a lanky boy who always twirled his pencil and dropped it as habitually, they were all my companions. Nearly every second was pregnant with redirection. I sat at my desk and wrote in my journal and wondered how much lower I could get.

Then I got lower, even if at first it seemed like I was ascending into heaven. I found a job at a group home in Nebraska, where I met someone who pole-vaulted in college. She had charcoal hair and thick lips, the kind men love because it reminds them of what happens in private. She grew up in the heart of Iowa but we were in the middle of nowhere in Nebraska and her presence solidified my belief that Christ had a plan for each and every one of us. That whole year working with her, I devoted myself to Him and to her. I listened when she told me one very late night about her ex-boyfriend who'd gone down on her, and who was baptized with her in a lake in Iowa. My faith wavered when she left without saying goodbye. It faltered when she emailed to tell me to stop worrying about her and to focus on Christ. It shattered when I moved to Sioux Falls and started working overnights at another group home in Sioux Falls while during the day loading trucks at UPS. Somewhere in the cracks I managed to meet Katherine from the burgeoning social media-focused internet. I knew, for sure this time, God had placedher in front of me on divine purpose. No other explanation would do. So I went to Alabama and tasted her manicured crotch and met her affluent family and attended her modern church with its video screens and rooms where tan college girls watched over toddlers. Those college girls wanted to be Katherine. It was like in high school, when I would stare at Brooke, unanimously known as the "hottest" in our high school as we stood in packs beside the concession stand, and instead of rolling her eyes this time she decided to change history and walk over and put her hand down my pants in the dead of winter and let me explore her body in the Deep South.

I left Katherine in balmy Alabama and arrived in the harshness of a Sioux Falls winter. Yes it was painful to leave my belle, my artist, my hippie who'd one day inherit her family's organic-grocery-store empire, but the message she sent the next morning took that hurt and hammered my hands to the cross. She wrote that what we had done was not God's will, and the plan we'd etched out while lying in her coffin of a bedroom on her soft mattress, with come rolling down her stomach, for me to live down the street from her and get a job as a writer, was no more. So I moved to Seattle. My dad warned against moving just because of a heartbreak, but to his surprise those first months I called home giddy. I'd found paradise and was not lost. I did not tell my parents, but without God, I was saved. Marriage was not imminent anymore. There were attractive women who wanted me and did not worry that if what we were doing was ordained in the Bible. I would not be alone. The package company had openings in management. I would not be poor.

Back at the hotel on my birthday after I told my parents the good news, after the hugs from my mother and the proudest looks I'd ever seen from my father, the women came. First, though, my father. Even as a boy, I remember, when I told him my dream of being a professional baseball player, he tried to dissuade me, as if trying to prepare me for adulthood. He never wanted me to be rich; he didn't want me to become conceited. He didn't want me to be poor either. He wanted me to be in the middle where I could live a respectable life, working at a job I maybe not loved but didn't hate, and even if I hated it, that's okay, as long as it provided for a family, though he never seemed to want me to have any girlfriends, just a wife, which I have to say now was a difficult task, to only have one and not the other. *My Father: A Difficult Man* might be his biography. He raised a sensitive son who invited two young women, one with red hair and the body of a yoga instructor, and another with sandy blonde hair who had the body of a Playboy Playmate, if paler, which only made me want her more. The only one missing was the curly-haired one, who I loved.

The two earthy ladies who recycled their eggshells in a compost bucket strolled into the hotel lobby in tank tops and sensible shorts as if they were modeling in a chaste but tantalizing show. They both gave me close hugs, pressing their breasts against me. If they hadn't been so Christian, and I hadn't been so stupid, we might have one day happened into a threesome. We stripped down to our suits and swam in the hotel pool in Tukwila under summer sunshine with hills and forest around us. I was too awe-struck, knowing they both wanted to be naked with me, to think about the curly-haired one or why I hadn't invited her. Maybe I was ashamed of having all three at one time, or I wanted to hide my dalliances with the two older ones —twenty-three and twenty-four—and once I was done with them and they had given me experience I would come back to Beth and we'd start a life together, because by then I'd have gotten my long-term job in package delivery management. All I can say is that after swimming, we celebrated my promotion and ate the pizza in air conditioning, wrapped in white towels. The girls' hair still damp, all of us delirious. Look at that, the Twins are winning. My mom was smiling. My dad was glad too, I could tell. He did not have to speak. I had seen his highs and lows. A first small spike on a graph trending upward, I thought then.

The next day my parents left and I got to work at my new job and I went about attempting to straighten out my situation with the three women. One weekend morning soon after I told Hannah, the redhead, as she straddled her bike in the driveway of my rented house, we'd be better off as friends, then I watched her go. The next weekend I held on to her as she convulsed like a dying animal. I calculated how many times I'd see such passion again, and it didn't seem like enough to not pursue my last remaining chances. Then I fumbled a clean handoff from Jenny, the more demure one with the blessed form. Just a week after she quietly accepted my offer to "just be friends," I called her to go to a rock show downtown, and afterward on the bus home I slipped my hand up her thigh under her skirt and she rested hers on my hardening prick. I then told Beth I had broken things off with Jenny and Hannah, and she hated me for how dramatic I'd made things, running away in the darkness of Gas Works Park. We had gone for a nighttime walk and she had straightened her hair. She wore a tank top and a sarong. The grass was wet. Later, I found her by the lake, cross-legged on a bench that was like a pew against the water. I held one of her sandals.

"I could have gotten that," she said. It had fallen off as she ran away.

"I know," I said, handing it to her. "Just thought I'd bring it to you."

We watched the city dance on the water. It must have been poetic enough that she forgave me. Jesus in Heaven makes up for all past anguish, I thought then, though I had stopped believing in God. I did not deserve such grace. But, like they teach in the Protestant churches, none of us do.

At my new job, the most common refrain from the drivers coming in at the end of their shift after clocking their DIAD into the slots was something along the lines of, "Good luck. You're going to need it," followed by obnoxious peals of sinister laughter. I shrugged, telling myself you have to go through some shit to get to where you want to go. Do work and good things will happen. The cards aren't stacked against you. They're out there, just waiting to be played. No one has a monopoly on the good ones. That's the kind of idiocy I believed then.

As context for the next part, my first experiences with bullying came in the seventh grade, in the year when the earth cracked and separated childhood from adolescence, causing a fracture whereby a few of us unlucky ones ended up on one side of the fault line—those of us who were softer, smellier, or more apt to cry—while the harder ones ended up on the other where they could not be touched. My crimes were obvious. My mom was a teacher at the high school and my head was oblong and my lisp hadn't totally gone away, even after years of speech therapy. To make matters worse, my sister was three years older and the "really hot," or so it was told to me by Lance, who asked me at football practice one summer during two-a-days if I filmed her nude in my family's home and masturbated to the tapes, because, as he said, "that's what I would do." As I got older, into ninth and tenth grade, I didn't have a car and was dropped off at school by my dad and walked in with mom. I didn't go out drinking in abandoned farmhouses, and I didn't chew or smoke. I wasn't all that good at sports, though going out for them and showering regularly did prevent me from being in the lowest caste. Still, I was given wedgies and threatened with violence or called E.T., a nickname from grade school. Garettewas the worst of the bunch, a heavyweight state champion wrestler who always reminded me of the sheriff from *Dukes of Hazzard and* who spit into an empty Mountain Dew bottle. Life got better when his class graduated at the end of my sophomore year and I became friends with the Mennonite kids from the private school. They didn't drink, and by my senior year I barely talked to anyone in my own class, even my best friend Nathan from youth, who had gotten into drugs and I began to have a harder time understanding him, like he had switched his radio to a different frequency. In the end, what I mean to say, I think what is important to say, is that Garette taught me that things can be bad but can get better.

In Seattle, I don't recall if I met Mike on my first day, though it couldn't have been long before he began to make every second at work miserable. I remember going to bed each night hoping Mike would die in some horrific manner. I imagined he picked up lonely divorcees at chain restaurants on weekends and that his condo was filled with leased appliances and tacky furniture bought brand-new from warehouse stores, that the only way he could orgasm was by choking small animals. It got so bad then that I could almost, if I looked away for a second, see the Garette's face as Mike's braying maw told me to stop "fucking the dog."

I did my best to keep up. I didn't turn away in faux modesty when the drivers took out their phones and showed me images of dead bodies or old men engaged in sex in hotel rooms. Mike didn't care what they watched or what they said to each other, as long as they completed their route on time and didn't waste any of the company's money. Mike was staunchly anti-union, and the only people he seemed to hate more than me were any of the drivers who meekly would add, as they fumbled to recite a worker's obligations from their union card, that they were entitled to a "fair day's work for a fair day's pay." Mike's response was always something like, "I am trying to run a business here." But for all his bravado, Mike would stammer and stutter during heated talks with the most obstinate drivers who would lope around and say they were "taking fifteen" and eventually, if that didn't work, go back out to help as instructed. When things got really bad and I could hear raised voices outside the concrete office building in the nook where the drivers got their delivery notice slips and checked their routes for the day, Mike would counter refusals with, "Okay then, I'll be writing you up," and though he had nothing to write up, it didn't matter. Mike was trying to get someone fired. It was the only thing that made him happy.

No matter the abuse, the job paid well enough and allowed me to continue living in a city with women with whom I shared important things in common. They loved simple pleasures like pho and British television shows and watching the Twins. They wanted to be naked and know me without an official relationship, something that could never have happened in Sioux Falls. They didn't wear makeup and were not concerned with money or their standing in the church. They had big breasts, or they orgasmed at the slightest touch, or they were twenty and had curly hair and wore striped underwear underneath jean skirts and smoked weed and rode longboards and laughed like they had no troubles. I was living a dream, not the bad kind where it's like intruding on someone's consciousness, but the good kind where time moves so quickly. I blinked and a month would be gone. Hannah found another, so there was only Jenny and Beth, and though Jenny had the most unreal body I knew I would ever encounter, it was not enough. I am sounding like a romance novelist, and not even a good one, but Beth was the one for me, and just when I realized that and decided to stop dragging my feet, she nearly died from a bike accident in the U District, slamming through the back window of a Subaru. I went that night after work to Swedish Medical Center to see her hooked up to tubes. Machines breathed for her. I held her hand. She squeezed back feebly and we were the closest we'd ever been, or would be.

For the next couple weeks I'd visit Beth after work and sit beside her. Her mom was there from Minnesota, and sometimes her bicycle-riding hippie friends would be there too. They'd see me at Beth's side when she'd reach out and we'd hold hands, but I could never look at Jenny as we did. Somewhere in there I asked Mike for time off after Christmas. He was putting away files, I remember, drinking a Diet Mountain Dew—a strange connection to Garette—wearing slinky slacks from Tommy Bahama, and I timidly asked, before the last drivers had returned, if I could go back home to South Dakota for the holidays. I wanted to show my family that I could be on my own and get a job without God's help and find a woman and make her happy without a legal contract. I was in Seattle and doing it and I wanted to show them what was possible, to bring Beth as a symbol of how much I had accomplished. There would be a scar on her cheek from rocketing through the back windshield of a Subaru wagon, and she might be a bit younger than appropriate, but she would be beautiful, and vibrant, and mine.

"We'll take care of you," was Mike's response. No, it didn't seem like enough, but I was glad I had mounted the courage to ask and considered his reply a stamped letter of approval. I booked my ticket.

Beth and I got closer then. After she regained her strength and could walk, she thanked me for coming to the hospital. Her mom had told her I had been there.

"You didn't have to do that," Beth said, "but thank you."

We were standing on a walkway above the cafeteria and the moment passed quickly. As I look back, I see we had lots of those fleeting specks, like tiny pieces of fiber, that she or mostly I, failed to gather. I should have grasped them, rolled them into a garment that clothed our connection and warmed a relationship. But I was scared Beth was too young, which is so stupid. Women mature faster than men. Also, though, and this will sound insane, I thought then, I can't tie myself down. I thought, Beth is perfect, so if she wants me, how many others will? I hadn't been in the city so long and I stood in awe of the bounty in the Pacific Northwest: Jenny, Hannah, and others I have not spoken of here. The only good thing I can say is after Beth got out of the hospital, I settled down. Her mom moved into her shared house with the hippies—I imagine she must have been very busy cleaning whenever not caring for her daughter—so I didn't stop by too often, afraid to appear not a gentleman, but Beth and I talked on the phone. Many nights she'd cry, thinking of her close call with death, or her face being scarred, or the thing that scared her the most, the hospital bill. In the end it got taken care of by way of leniency from the hospital through a program that assisted people like Beth who never thought they'd be in such a situation, and she became less worried, and she laughed more, recalling the details others told her while she was on the pain medications. And though the scar on her cheek was sizable, she'd someday get plastic surgery, even if I told her I liked how tough it made her look. I didn't tell Beth about Mike. Someday, I thought, I'd move up and know so much about the package delivery business I could support her and pay for her college, along with any remaining bills from her accident, and she would never have to know a thing about him. But then it all began to unravel. Beth went north to Bellingham for college. She'd been in Seattle for a year building houses, and her parents bought her a used wagon that looked very safe and sturdy, and her mom and I helped Beth pack up one Friday. It was early afternoon before my shift at UPS, and Wallingford was quiet and gray, with that distinct smell of Seattle in the air, the nostalgic one you can't forget if you ever lived there. Beth's mom called her down to go, and I remember thinking, this is it, I have to tell her everything now. All I did was give her a mix of songs we both liked on a CD. Beth kissed me goodbye.

There were visits. One came before Halloween, when she told me as I drove to my place from the bus stop she planned on going as one of those petrified heads, since her jaw was all wired up from the accident. Later, her on top, she said she was sorry she couldn't do what she normally did. A month later I remember watching her park her green wagon on the street by my shared commune of a house. She wore no more bandages and a new skirt with a black blouse and a red necklace. She brought with her a movie her new roommates loved—which I knew meant she was becoming closer to them—and we watched it on my bed and she laughed her laugh that seemed only for me and this time we could do the old things. Afterward she got up from the bed, took the lone candle from my desk, and in one motion curled her finger. It is her long back, her ass jutting out, that cripples me now thinking about. She beckoned me to the bathroom, where she finished me in the dim romantic light. I still think about that. Only once did I go up to see her in Bellingham, in the part of the country that looks like you've stepped into Middle Earth, but she did not laugh her laugh, and her welcoming posture was gone. We had a very short visit before she said she had work to do, which she had never said before. Going home that day I actually thought her pulling away was the best thing possible.

Like Saunders says, there comes a time in life when, tired of losing, you keep on losing, and when that time of losing comes to an end you think, this time, this time I'll stop losing. For years I drifted around, trying to find others like Beth, but I never did. I saw Jenny from time to time, but only when we were too lonely. Hannah's red hair was nice as well intermittently, but when the shaking ended and she got dressed I knew she'd soon be out looking for someone more stable. One year around Easter, Mike left for another part of the building and it wasn't nearly the momentous occasion I once dreamed his leaving would be. I became insignificant, not moving up and staying a dispatcher.

Sometimes, though, while waiting for the last of the drivers to trickle in, I'll be alone in my concrete-block office that has grime on the walls and the dry-erase board with the names of the drivers behind me, and I'll be finished with my Coke and instant soup with

Bugles, and I'll rub my nearly totally bald head and be reminded of a time long ago. That first winter after the accident and just a few weeks after I visited her in Bellingham, when I could tell Beth was trying to say goodbye, I went home and saw my family, but when I got there I got a call from Mike. He screamed that I needed to get right back to Seattle or I'd lose my job. I hadn't gotten the right clearance for the time off, he said. So I returned, since I was a coward, and my whole plan came apart. I had plotted to see Beth. With two weeks off, I thought I could take one of them to surprise her. Drive my parents' car and go to northern Minnesota. Maybe, I thought then, the gesture would show her how much I suddenly and irreversible felt. But with the trip cut short, I couldn't, so I went back to Seattle, and Beth returned to Seattle the next spring with a boyfriend.

In another timeline I imagine now Beth on my arm, her hair still curly, both of us are in formalwear and on our way to a gala. We need to stop at work to grab some papers first. But my office isn't the same drab office on the first floor. Now it's on a higher story, with clear windows so all the workers have to look up to see me. By now I have learned a lot about package delivery management and have told Mike where he can stick it. We walk into the building, skipping security, and Mike sees me with my new wife, who is a local celebrity for her work as an environmental activist— possibly because she is so pretty—and though he can remember the beginning, when I was a timid dispatcher with no experience, he can't help but stutter when he says his own name. However, Beth is generous. She does not belittle him, and as we walk away we both can sense Mike watching us go.

Then one of the last drivers comes in and the daydream breaks, and I hear the coughing of another truck leaving or coming, and the whir of the belt moving the packages, and the beating of my stupid heart.

Acknowledgements

Thank you to all who have read these stories in their different forms over the last many years. And thank you Kristin, for the editing, and Elizabeth, once again thank you for the fine cover. And to my wife: I love you and you are lovely.

www.ingramcontent.com/pod-product-compliance
Lightning Source LLC
Chambersburg PA
CBHW021150130626
46554CB00005B/1742